MR. OCTOBER

Calendar Boys Series

NICOLE S. GOODIN

Mr. October
Published by Nicole S. Goodin
ISBN: 978-0-9951276-3-0
Copyright 2019 by Nicole S. Goodin
All rights reserved. ©
First published October 2019

Cover design by Nicole Goodin
Images purchased from Shutterstock
Editing by Spell Bound

For all the babes born in October

CHAPTER ONE

Masen

"Are you even listening to me, Masen?"

I catch my name at the end of the sentence and roll my head lazily in the direction of Ange, my PR chick.

She really needs to get laid; the woman's always bitching about something.

"Well?" she demands as our eyes meet.

I shrug. I don't know what the hell she's going on about. I don't really care either.

"He's not even listening to me," she hisses, turning her attention to Chuck, my manager. "I don't know how you've lasted this long with him."

I yawn. A barely concealed threat to quit, *again*.

I debate telling her to just go, but then I'd have to hire someone else, and that sounds like a lot of work.

Chuck shoots me a look that tells me he needs me to help him the fuck out.

If it were anyone else, I'd probably ignore them, but I've got a soft spot for Chuck. He's the only person in this building that still sees me as a person and not just someone they can make a shit load of money from.

"I'm listening," I drawl. "*Talk*."

She scowls at me, straightens her already perfectly put together folder and starts talking.

"We need to sort out your image; going to rehab has really hit your sales hard."

I interject, "I don't think the *rehab* was the problem."

She clicks her tongue. Nothing gets a PR chick riled up faster than referring to a PR nightmare situation, and shit, do I have a few of those under my belt.

"Regardless," she replies tightly, "your sales are down, and your reputation has gone to the dogs."

I snort out a bitter laugh. *To the dogs*. She talks like she's old as fuck when I doubt she's much more than ten years older than me. I've slept with women older than her.

"I'm the prick of the year, I get it. What do you want me to do about it?"

"Clean up your act," she replies swiftly.

I raise a brow at her. "I thought that's what I was doing in rehab."

Her eyes soften, but only a fraction. I know deep down she's thankful as hell that I've kicked the bottle, but I've made her life a living hell for the past two years, aged her at least ten years I reckon; it's going to take more than a thirty-day programme to get in her good graces.

"It's going to take a bit more effort than that I'm afraid."

I rake my hand over my face. Of course it is. Nothing is ever enough – it's always more. "What are you thinking?"

I'm not sure I care what it is, and I'm in no way indicating I'm about to actually follow through with any of it, I just want to get out of here so I can light up a smoke already. It's the only bad habit I was allowed to keep.

"We're going to start booking you in for public appearances again... events, red carpets, that kind of thing. We need the media and your peers to see Masen Lennox, *sober*."

"Whatever." I wave my hand at her. "Is that it?"

She shakes her head. "No. Chuck and I think it would benefit you greatly, publicly and privately, if you had a woman in your life."

I smirk at her. "What makes you think there aren't women in my life?"

"*Woman*." she snaps at me. "*Singular*. A girlfriend, not a bunch of bed-hopping hoes."

My mouth twitches in amusement. I've never heard her say the word 'hoes'.

"I don't do girlfriends."

She looks to Chuck for help and he leans forward, resting his elbows on his knees, pinning me with his stare. "*Look*, I'm going to level with you, kid, the label still wants to drop you."

Well shit.

My expression remains the same – static, *unflinching*, but he nods, knowing that I understand how serious this is.

I thought rehab would have placated them, apparently, I was wrong.

"Either you clean up your act, or you're gone."

"When we mentioned that you'd settled down with a nice girl, it really seemed to go a long way," Ange cuts in.

I groan. "You've already told them I've got a chick."

I'm fucked. They've fucked me over with this. They've backed me into a corner, and they know it.

I don't do girlfriends and I'm not about to start now, so if I want to keep my career intact, it looks like I'm going to have to pretend.

Chuck glares at her before turning back to me, his mind already in line with mine.

"We can hire a pro – an escort or something, string it out for a few months, maybe even a year and pay her well enough that she doesn't breathe a word to anyone," he offers.

"And what happens when one of her previous clients recognises her? Takes it public? That might be worse than getting shitfaced and spewing on the red carpet."

He grimaces.

He's right, it probably *wouldn't* be worse, but whatever.

"We'll bring someone in from out of town, hell, out of country if we have to."

"Just stop," I tell him. "Let me think for a god damn minute."

My gaze wanders for the first time, through the huge glass walls and out into the offices surrounding us.

They're really doing a great job of making me feel closed in; people from my label are literally all around us.

Producers, assistants, secretaries, interns... they're all here, and they're probably all judging me too.

Not that I give a shit. As long as I can make music, I don't give a shit about any of that.

I linger on a girl with long brown hair; she's delivering coffee to some record label douche.

He waves her away with his hand after she sits the cup down in front of him, and I don't miss the 'fuck you' look plastered across her face. I definitely don't miss when she raises her middle finger at the back of his head before rushing away, her fine ass swaying.

"*If* I'm going to do this, *I* want to choose the girl," I bargain.

"Within reason," Ange replies. "She can't look like you found her on the street corner."

"We do this my way," I say, ignoring her insult to my taste in women.

"We'll see."

That's the best I'm going to get out of this uptight bitch.

I nod my head slowly as I consider it. I can pretend. I can play make believe for a few months to save my career – the only thing I still care about.

"Alright," I reply, my eyes still watching the brunette. "I'll do it."

"Excellent. I'll start compiling a list of possible candidates," Ange says, her relieved voice coming from up above me as she gets to her feet. Always so efficient.

"No need," I say, twisting back to face the two of them.

Chuck frowns and Ange's brows knit together. "But you said…"

"I said, *I'll* choose the girl."

"Okay…" Ange replies, still confused. "Well then, where is she?"

I turn my shoulder and point to the harmless looking brunette who appears to come with a side of sass. "Right there. I want *her*."

CHAPTER TWO

Billie

"Billie, Ms. Steel wants to see you in the conference room."

"*Who* does?" I reply, panicked.

I've done my best to remember all the names and faces of every person that works in this building, but the name Steel is drawing a total blank.

Christina peers back at me like I'm a moron. "The blonde chick in there with Masen Lennox." She tips her head towards the glass-walled room in the centre of this floor.

I swallow slowly. "She wants me to go in the same room as *Masen Lennox?*"

She pops her gum and chews it noisily – quite possibly the most annoying trait she possesses. "Yip. Sure does."

I wring my hands together nervously. "Do they want coffee?"

"How the hell should I know, I'm just passing on a message."

"Do *you* think I should take coffee?"

"Just go in the room, *Jesus*, you need to chill," she snaps.

I gape after her as she stalks away, off to be a bitch to someone else, no doubt.

She's just told me to go into a room containing one of the most famous singers in the entire world, and she expects me to swan on in like it's no big deal at all.

Knowing he was in the building this morning is the reason I nearly dropped a tray of coffees on the floor.

It's also the reason I've not once looked in the direction of that conference room.

They've failed to use the privacy screens the whole time they've been in there, which only makes it more unnerving. It's easier to forget him if I can't see him.

I step around the corner, away from the copier I've been hiding out at and glance nervously at my destination.

Three sets of eyes are on me, waiting.

The tall blonde woman waves at me, indicating for me to come over. She looks both impatient and unimpressed.

Great.

I nod once at her, avoiding the two men at all costs.

I walk on shaky legs towards the door.

The other man in the room is Chuck Brown – Masen Lennox's manager. He's been with him since before his sudden rise to fame. Whispers around the office are that he's the only person Masen really gives a shit about disappointing, and I bet he's been doing a lot of that this past year.

I reach for the handle and will the tremor in my fingers to go away.

I'm just an intern. I've only been here a few months. I knew I'd see famous musicians from time to time, but I don't have a clue what one of the biggest names in music could possibly want with me.

I pull the door open, the whoosh of air making me even more nervous.

"Billie, please come in," the woman says.

Christina said her name was Ms. Steel – I hope like hell she was right.

"Of course, Ms. Steel," I reply as I rush into the room, still avoiding the other sets of eyes I can feel on my face.

She looks at me curiously. "Call me Ange." She points to a seat for me to sit in.

"Ange," I say quietly as I sit down.

"This is Chuck Brown." She points to the man sitting opposite me, and I finally lift my eyes to his.

He's seriously hot for an older dude. "Hi," I breathe.

He nods once at me, his expression tight. I get the impression he doesn't like whatever it is that I'm here for any more than Ange does.

"And I'm sure you've heard of Masen," Ange offers.

I swallow deeply and shift my gaze from the handsome older man to the scorching hot younger one next to him.

"Hello, Billie," he says, his voice throaty and delicious.

I suck in a breath. Masen Lennox just said my name. *Holy shit.*

"Hey... hi... I'm a big fan."

Chuck groans. "This is *never* going to work."

"Shut up," Masen hisses.

Ange looks sceptical.

I suddenly feel like an animal in a zoo as they take turns appraising me.

"Ummm... sorry, but *why* am I here?" I shift my stare between Chuck and Ange, being careful not to extend it to Masen.

"I've got a... *proposition* for you." It's Masen who replies, and I'm forced to look at him again.

God, he's gorgeous in that 'I don't give a shit' kind of way; mussed dark hair, faded black t-shirt with a tear in the neckline, and ripped black jeans. His shoes are scuffed-up black chucks that he rocks in a way only a superstar can.

His brown eyes roam over my face and just the action alone makes my skin break out in goosebumps.

"I'm sure you've heard about Masen's recent stint in rehab," Ange cuts in, taking over the explanation.

I nod. The whole world heard about his alcohol addiction.

"Ninety days sober," Masen drawls, and I get the impression he's not all that happy about it.

Ange shoots him a glare.

"Now, I'm not sure what it is you do here..."

"I'm an intern," I provide.

"Right... well, you're probably not aware of the impact Masen's past indiscretions have had on his career."

"I'm hardly surprised." The words are out of my mouth before I can stop them, and I curse myself internally. I can't believe I just said that out loud.

My eyes flicker to Masen and he smirks, seemingly unfazed by my comment.

Ange narrows her eyes for a moment, before launching back into her explanation.

"Long story short, Billie, Masen needs to clean up his act, get some of his wholesome image back."

I almost laugh. There is nothing much wholesome about Masen Lennox – he's a bad boy through and through. I doubt there's anything or anyone in the world that could change that.

"And we think the best way forward is for Masen to have a young woman in his life."

"Okay..." I reply, confused by where this conversation is going.

"But the problem is –"

"The problem is, I don't do girlfriends," Masen interjects.

I nod. "Okay... noted?" I still have no idea why I'm in here, involved in this obviously personal chat.

"So, we're looking to hire someone, Billie, do you understand?"

I nod slowly, I still can't quite believe this is happening. "So... you want me to make a list or something? I can do that."

"We were thinking more along the lines of –"

"Oh for fuck's sake, stop beating around the bush," Masen interrupts her. "I want *you* to be my girlfriend."

I feel my jaw fall lax. "I'm sorry, what?" I point at myself. "*Me?*"

He leans forward in his seat, his elbows resting on his knees, his hands clasped in front of him, lean muscles bulging against the confines of his shirt.

"Be my girl?"

I blink slowly, totally transfixed by his beautiful face, his sexy mouth speaking words I never in a million years thought I'd hear directed at me.

"But... but... you don't even know me," I stutter.

He shrugs one of his shoulders. "Not important."

"But..."

He cuts me off before I have the chance to speak again.

"You're hot as fuck, you seem sweet, what more do I need to know?"

Masen Lennox just said I was 'hot as fuck'.

Holy. Fucking. Shit.

"I don't think I'm the right girl for the job. I'm shy. I'm boring."

"Trust me, sugar, there's nothing boring about you."

Another shiver passes over my skin. He just called me sugar, and I'm practically putty in his hands.

This is definitely a bad idea.

"What about Christina? She's confident and sexy..."

"Christina could work," Ange chimes in, her tone hopeful.

"No," he replies sternly. "It's her or no one."

I see Ange and Chuck exchange a wary glance.

"I... I'm... I don't know what to say."

"*Yes* would be good," Masen replies.

"Why? *Why* would I do that?"

I didn't intend to voice that question aloud, but apparently my mouth didn't get the memo.

"How does a million dollars sound?" he replies lazily, leaning back against his seat, casual as anything, like he didn't just offer me a shit load of money to be his fake girlfriend.

"Jesus Christ, Masen," Chuck growls.

"Oh my goodness." Ange gasps.

"*What*?" Masen shrugs, unfazed. "If she's going to have to live with my ass for the next however long, she deserves to be paid well."

A *million* dollars.

I feel like I'm going to puke.

"*Live with*?" I question, my voice no more than a harsh whisper.

"No woman of mine would be living anywhere but with me," he says, alpha rolling off him in waves.

"I think we need to discuss this arrangement in private," Chuck insists.

Masen waves him away, his eyes still fixed on mine. "You're up for it, right, Billie?" His voice caresses my name and my insides turn to mush.

No, my brain tells me. NO. I'm not up for it at all.

So when my mouth opens and I reply, "*yes*," I think I'm more shocked than anyone else.

***

"You're going to need to slow down and start again from the beginning," Avery demands, talking to me like I'm a small child losing the plot.

I suck in a shallow breath.

"I need you to sign this." I thrust the neat stack of papers in her direction.

"What's this?" She frowns.

"It's an NDA; I promised you'd sign it before I told you anything."

"But you just told me stuff and I haven't signed it yet."

"Just sign it!" I reply quickly, my voice rising an octave.

She rolls her eyes and grabs a pen. "Fine, fine, calm your tits."

I pace the room as she flicks through the papers, signing a non-disclosure agreement, similar to the one I signed earlier today. Ange put little colour-coded sticky tabs on every spot she needs to sign.

She drops the pen. "There, *done*, now take a deep breath and tell me what the hell is going on."

I do as she's asked, taking a long, deep breath, in through my nose and out through my mouth.

Avery has been my best friend for years, and my roommate since we finished high school. Neither of us were dorm kind of girls, so we got a flat together, close to campus.

I'm still pacing the room as I breathe.

"Sit," she demands, "You're making me jumpy."

I fall into the closest chair.

"I got called into a room with Masen Lennox, his manager, and his PR lady, right?"

"Right."

"They want Masen to clean up his public image, after, you know..."

"After he became a total ass and drank himself into a stupor?" she offers.

I wouldn't have been quite so harsh, but she's not exactly wrong about it either. The guy really hit rock bottom for a while there.

"Essentially, yeah..."

She nods. "And how exactly do *you* fit into this?"

"They think he needs a girlfriend... well, a fake one anyway, so it looks like he's sober and getting on with his life."

"Hold up. *Looks like* he's sober?"

"I mean, he is sober." I roll my eyes. "That doesn't give him a squeaky-clean image just yet, but he's off the booze."

"You sure?"

I nod. "Ninety days and counting."

She seems satisfied by that answer, and I'm thankful we can move on, whether or not he's still drinking isn't even the bit blowing my mind.

"So the girlfriend...?"

I sigh. "That's apparently where *I* come in. *I'm* the girl-friend."

Her eyes widen and she blinks, once, twice, three times without speaking.

"I know, right?" I drop my head back against the couch and shut my eyes. "It's a complete clusterfuck."

"How? Why? *What*?" she stutters.

"My thoughts exactly." I groan, sitting back up to look at my gaping best friend. "He just pointed to the nearest female I think, and before I knew it, he was offering me a million dollars to play along and calling me *hot as fuck*."

"What the actual hell?"

I nod furiously. "*I know*... and then he said he wouldn't do it with anyone but me, and I don't know, I felt responsible for his reputation or something."

"A million dollars?" she questions, ignoring my rambling.

I nod. "That's what he said."

"And you said yes?"

"What would you have said?" I raise my brows at her.

She grins wickedly. "I probably would have done it without the million bucks."

"You *just* said he was an ass."

She nods. "He is, but *god* he looks good doing it."

I huff out a laugh. Can't argue with that.

We sit in silence for a few beats, both of us absorbing this information.

"Did you just become Masen Lennox's private hooker?"

"I think I did."

I'm pretty sure the million-dollar contract sitting on my kitchen table makes it legit.

"Do you have to... you know?" She makes a circle with one of her hands and pokes her finger through.

I glare at her, outraged. "There is *no* way I'm having sex with him."

"You say that now..."

"This is purely business."

She snorts. "*Purely business*, in no way influenced by the sex appeal of your new business partner?"

I shake my head, lying to myself. "Nope."

She snorts out a laugh. "Alright then."

"All I have to do is live at his house, go places with him and act like I'm in love. No big deal."

"Hold the phone, *live* with him?"

I clear my throat. "Um, so yeah... turns out I have to live at his place."

"Because *that* sounds like a normal relationship progression," she replies, sarcasm dripping from her tone.

"The story is that we've been seeing each other in private since he got out of rehab."

"Of course you have."

We stare at one another for a few seconds.

"This was a terrible idea, wasn't it?" I groan.

"I think it might have been, but hey, it might be fun... and it's not like the view will be bad... ooooh, you should see if he'll buy you new clothes and stuff."

"You *would* be thinking about free shit."

"Uh, *yeah*," she replies as though it was a stupid thing to doubt.

I hide my face in my hands. "I'm not cut out for this. Why couldn't he have picked you out of a crowd? You'd be perfect."

"I'm not sure if that's a compliment or if you just d-low called me a hooker…"

I groan again. I can't believe this is really happening.

"They want me there this afternoon."

"Well, you better get packing… Are you allowed to have sleepovers in his mansion? Because I'm going to need to see it with my own eyes."

I drop my hands to my lap and shake my head. "You really think I can pull this off?"

She nods. "You've got this. Just be careful, B, a guy like Masen Lennox could chew up and spit out a sweet girl like you."

I sigh.

Don't I know it.

CHAPTER THREE

Masen

"Don't look at me like that, this was your fucking idea. You and Ange can only blame yourselves when this goes to shit."

"I thought you'd hire a pro," Chuck grumbles, "Not pick up some fucking intern... and a million dollars? Are you sure you're not drinking again?"

I glare at him.

I'm all too fucking sure.

I'd kill for a drink right now, but I won't have one.

Even *I* can see that alcohol and me don't go well together, but that doesn't make me crave it any less.

"She's going to be here in five minutes, why don't you fuck off with the pacing?"

He flips me off, and I chuckle under my breath.

"What are you freaking out about now? It's just a chick. Maybe we should have got you one too. Might have got you to relax a bit."

"Got another mil lying around, do you?"

"Matter of fact, I do."

"You're such an arrogant prick."

"Doesn't make it any less true."

"You know what? I thought the price tag was unreasonable, but now I'm starting to wonder if you should have offered her double that to put up with you."

I waggle my brows. "I might just offer performance-based incentives."

He narrows his eyes at me. "Don't even fucking think about it. This isn't some groupie chick that's down for the game, this is an innocent little girl."

"She's hardly a little girl."

"She's still technically a fucking teenager, Masen, I know you're young too, but shit, this girl is a *normal* young. She hasn't been exposed to the world you live in, and you're going to have to try and shield her as much as possible."

I wave him off. She's a grown woman for fuck's sake, I'm not going to be holding her hand – not unless we're in public anyway.

I'm not going to be sleeping with her either, no matter what I might say to Chuck. You don't mix business with pleasure. I know that. And besides, she's sweet. Sweet isn't my thing.

"Seriously, Masen – *don't*. She'll fall in love with you and you'll crush her, I can see it coming."

I scowl at him.

"Because I'm so fucking charming?" I snap sarcastically.

"Hasn't deterred the rest of the female population."

Fuck that. They only like the idea of me. There's not a woman in the world who really knows me and that's not about to change.

"Sir, your guest has arrived." Morris appears behind me, startling me. He's always fucking sneaking around.

"I need to get you a collar with a bell on it," I mutter.

"I'd really prefer if you didn't."

"Did you let her in?"

He nods. "Yes, Sir. I'll give you a moment to get acquainted while I take her bags up to her room."

"Oh, you're not going to make her share your bed too? How fucking noble of you," Chuck drawls.

"I thought I told you to fuck off," I hiss as her car comes into view.

I do a double take out the window at the piece of shit car that just parked in my driveway.

Chuck laughs. "Bad luck, looks like you're going to be buying a new set of wheels."

"She can take her pick out of the garage," I mutter, unconcerned.

A car is the least of my worries.

I watch as she climbs out of the car and stretches her arms high above her head, her top riding up to reveal her tanned, toned stomach. She's wearing the shortest shorts known to man and her long legs are on full display.

"*Christ*," I say on an exhale.

So much for sweet not being my thing.

Her being here might all be an act, but the sudden urge I have to fuck her is as real as they come.

Fuck.

She strolls around to her boot and pops it open before lugging out a huge suitcase which she promptly drops to the ground near her sneaker-clad foot.

She obviously doesn't realise we have help for that.

"Fuck's sake," I growl as she pulls out another huge bag and glances up at the house.

"Morris!" I yell, "She's piling shit all over the drive. Can you take care of it?"

"Certainly, Sir," he calls back. I hear the front door open and then I see him rushing out towards her, yelling to her that he'll sort it out for her.

She smiles brightly at him, and I scowl.

"Go and get her you little prick." Chuck shoves my shoulder.

"I'll tell you what," I bargain, "I'll go and bring her in, as long as you're gone by the time I get back."

"Try not to break her," he mumbles before walking away to leave out back.

I run my hand through my hair and try to dull the urge I have to jump in my car and head for the nearest bar.

I can do this.

I *have* to do this.

I can tolerate a woman in my house for a few months.

I can get my shit back together.

Morris points her in the direction of the house, and I cuss. "Looks like I haven't got any fucking choice anyway," I hiss to myself.

***

"That's your room." I point inside the room and she looks in with interest. "Morris will have all your shit in there soon."

"Where's your room?"

I point up. "Third storey. I don't really use this level, so it's all yours."

She nods, her head bobbing up and down, her long, wavy hair spilling around her shoulders.

Brunettes aren't even my type, but there was just something about this girl that felt right from the second I laid eyes on her – like she was the only girl for the job. Seeing her here, in my house, that feeling has intensified tenfold.

She wanders along behind me. I pause at the bottom of the stairs that lead up to my room, considering taking her up, but think better of it.

"You won't need to go up there."

She nods. "Okay."

I pass the staircase and head down the hall, then back downstairs and out back into the yard.

I point. "Pool. Sauna. Gym."

"You have a gym *and* a sauna?" she asks, her tone impressed.

I glance over my shoulder at her. She's a lot less tongue-tied today.

"Got a recording studio and a bowling lane in the basement too."

Her eyes light up. "You're kidding?"

"Do I look like I make jokes?"

She lifts one of her shoulders. "I don't feel qualified to answer that yet."

I eye her curiously. The 'yet' on the end of that sentence concerns me.

"Right... well... Morris is here if you need anything, dinner is at seven, and if you see a blonde dude roaming around, it's just Josh, a mate of mine... sometimes he crashes in the pool house."

"Alright." She nods, her gaze wandering around the outdoor area. "So, what do you want me to do now?"

"Whatever the fuck you want," I reply lazily.

She frowns at me, her warm hazel eyes confused. "What do you mean? You're paying me to be here, and what? I'm just meant to relax by the pool?"

I shrug as I turn to walk back inside. "When we're not in public, I couldn't care less what you do."

I hear her following me. "I'm still allowed to go to classes, right?"

"Just told you, sugar, don't care. As long as nothing you do reflects badly on me, then we're good."

Her hand lands on my bicep, and I stop walking, spinning around to face her.

Her hand drops like I've given her an electric shock. "Sorry, I... um... I..."

There she goes, fucking stuttering again.

"I just don't see what the point of me being here is."

I reach out and grasp a handful of her long hair. I tug it gently and she gasps. "The *point*, is that tomorrow, our relationship is going to be 'leaked' to the press, and if you weren't here with me, you'd get hounded. As it is, you're going to have to make some changes."

Her eyes widen as they trail from my hand, up my arm to meet my gaze.

She looks worried. It's like she never considered what any of this would mean for her life.

There's a reason I felt compelled to offer her a million dollars.

"What kind of changes?" she whispers.

"A new car for starters." I drop her hair and turn, walking away again. "A new wardrobe, a bodyguard... you name it, sugar."

I'm in the doorway when she calls after me, "Masen!"

I stop, but don't look back; her curiosity is exhausting me. I don't have the patience to play babysitter. That's what Morris is for.

I expect more rapid-fire questions, but what I get surprises me. "Why do you keep calling me 'sugar'?"

"Because you're too fucking sweet."

CHAPTER FOUR

Billie

I reach for my phone from the sun lounger next to me.

I feel like all I've done for two days is work on my tan.

Masen excused me from my internship at the record label, and as much as that pissed me off, I have to admit it has been nice to have nowhere to be for an entire weekend.

He wasn't joking about it when he said my life was going to blow up once they leaked our story to the press.

They dug up my old high school pictures to print in gossip magazines, my Instagram followers are now in the hundreds of thousands, my Facebook friend requests went so wild I had to deactivate my account, and reporters kept calling my old phone number to the point where I tossed it in the pool.

Morris got me an expensive new phone, brand new sim card, and if I thought that was overwhelming, it was nothing compared to when he took me to the garage and told me to choose a new car to drive. Apparently, it was *Mr. Lennox's* request that I travel in style.

I've barely seen Masen since he showed me around. We've eaten dinner together each night, but considering he makes a living writing music and singing, he sure doesn't say much.

I don't know if it's a good thing or a bad thing – he makes me nervous, but I also feel a bit ripped off spending all my time on my own – I'm not sure how I'm meant to pretend I'm in love with him if I don't know a single thing about him.

I type out a text to Avery. She's been begging to visit me, but I'm not ready for that yet. Avery is like a wrecking ball, and I don't even really know what I'm dealing with here. I'm not ready for her to turn up and ruffle everyone's feathers.

To: Avery
  From: Billie
  Such a tough life

I attach a picture of my bare legs and the ridiculously lavish pool beyond.

She texts back with the emoji of a hand pulling the middle finger.

I sigh and scroll through my kindle app, looking for a book to catch my attention.

I'm *bored*.

I could go and see what Morris is doing, but honestly, I don't think he knew what to say when I offered to help him do the washing or clean the house yesterday.

This arrangement is not what I imagined it would be.

I'm not sure exactly what I *did* imagine, but it wasn't sitting by the pool, bored out of my mind, all alone.

I glance around and try to listen for any noise.

I assume Masen is in the basement, in his studio. I saw him go down there a few hours ago, and I haven't seen him come up again.

I also haven't heard a thing, so it must be soundproof. Either that, or he's bowling – but I just can't picture him doing that.

I'm dying to go down there and find out, but I feel like I'm invading his privacy. I thought he might have invited me in by now, but he hasn't. In fact, he hasn't shown me a single thing around here since I first arrived. He's barely glanced in my direction if I'm honest.

I guess his comments about me being 'hot as fuck' were designed to get me to agree to be his pretend girlfriend rather than being genuine, because he's clearly not in the least bit fazed by my presence.

I toss my phone back down, having no luck with the book search, and I'm just about to go back inside to find something to eat when I hear feet running, coming up behind me.

"Fire in the hole!" a voice bellows, and I curl up into myself, having no idea what's coming for me.

I see a shadow leap and then a huge splash lands water all over me.

"Shit!" I shriek, grabbing for my phone and drying it off with a towel. I seem to recall Morris telling me something about it being waterproof, but you can't be too careful.

A head pops up in the centre of the pool and shakes another spray of water in my direction.

A grinning, blonde-haired guy slides his arms through the water gracefully until he's resting his elbows on the side of the pool right in front of me.

"*Damn*, when he told me he had a fake girlfriend, I thought he meant a blow-up doll or something."

I grimace. "That's gross."

He presses up, his biceps bulging as he levers himself out of the pool, water dripping off his bare torso and down his board-shorts.

Sweet lord.

This guy is in seriously good shape.

"I'm Josh," he states, still grinning a boyish grin, a deep dimple in his left cheek.

Wow.

I swallow deeply. "Billie," I manage to reply.

His eyes roam over my bikini-clad body, making no attempt to hide his ogling.

I'm torn between covering myself up and taking off the little I *am* wearing.

I don't know where that brazen thought came from, it's not like me at all, but this stranger's stare is heating me up.

He finishes his eye fuck, his gaze meeting mine again.

"Where is the grumpy fucker?"

I shrug. "I don't seem to see him much."

"Rude prick," he says, shaking his hair out again. "C'mon, FG, we're going to find him."

He holds out his hand to me and before I can even make sense of what's happening, I take his hand in mine.

He pulls me to my feet, tugging me closer to him than is in any way required, his body hitting against mine.

He's tall and broad and cut and *gorgeous.*

Oh man.

He's absolutely cut to shreds.

Jesus. What have I got myself into?

I've barely had a chance to speak to a male since starting college, let alone one that looks like this, and the ones I left behind in high school were just boys... but not Josh here. No... he's *all* man.

"FG?" I question, my tongue darting out to moisten my lips.

My hand is still in his and his other hand is resting on my elbow now, I'm not even sure when that happened.

"*Fake* girlfriend," he murmurs, emphasising the word 'fake'.

"Right." I nod, my throat thick.

He's looking down at me like he wants to kiss me.

I don't know who this guy is, but his complete and utter confidence is magnetising. I can't look away.

His hand trails from my elbow, up my arm to cup my neck.

Holy shit. What the fuck is going on here?

"Get your man-whore hands off my girl," Masen's deep voice sounds from behind me and I gasp, my belly fluttering at the sound of his no-bullshit tone.

Josh chuckles, and just like that the spell is broken.

His hand drops from my neck and he steps back a fraction, dropping my hand and slinging his wet arm around my shoulders instead.

"If you're not going to play with her, I will." Josh chuckles.

I nudge him in the ribs. "What makes you think I want to play with you, jackass?"

"Didn't hear too many complaints a minute ago."

I feel my cheeks heat. He's right. I wasn't putting up much of a fight.

I try to shrug out of his hold, but he doesn't let me.

"Can you get your hands off her? Fuck's sake, man, I can't leave you alone for thirty seconds," Masen growls, and I finally manage to get free as Josh chuckles.

I don't know why I feel like I've been caught doing something wrong, I mean, kissing strangers isn't exactly my normal past time, but Masen told me to do 'whatever the fuck I wanted' while I was here, so it's not like he could be mad if I had done it.

I would have thought that Josh was classed as 'whatever the fuck I want', but the look on Masen's face is giving the distinct impression that this is not the case.

He's made it abundantly clear that he doesn't give a shit what I get up to, but right now, it seems like he does care after all, maybe just a tiny bit.

I reach for my towel and try to wrap it around my body. When I chose this skimpy bikini this morning, I planned to be the only person to see it, and now it feels like all eyes are on me.

Josh snags it from my hand and runs it through his soaked hair instead.

"Sorry, FG, I'm all wet," he says, his tone confirming that he's not sorry at all.

I grumble a series of curse words under my breath.

"Didn't catch that, sorry, were you telling me how wet *you* were?"

My eyes bulge, and he erupts into laughter, tossing the now-damp towel back to me.

"*Jesus*, your face." He sniggers, turning back to Masen, who is watching us with an unamused expression. "Where'd you find this one, bro? She embarrasses easy. I like her."

I hurriedly cover myself with the towel, my face flaming.

"Fuck off into the house, would you," Masen tells Josh, who laughs again, but complies, as he strolls towards the door.

"Good luck, FG," he calls over his shoulder. "Don't let him bite."

I don't exactly know what I need good luck for, but the barely concealed irritation on Masen's face tells me I'm about to find out.

He walks towards me, his lazy, languid steps a stark contrast to the tension radiating from him.

"I should have warned you about Josh," he says as he comes to a stop right in front of me, closer than he's ever been before.

I tug the towel higher up my chest. "Oh, um... I mean you told me he'd be here sometimes..."

He glances over his shoulder, back at the house, and I see a frown on his face.

"He's a player."

"Okay..." I reply warily. I'm not exactly sure why I'm being warned off his best friend, but I think that's *exactly* what's happening here.

"I'll have a word with him."

"Um... about what?" I question. I squint as I try to look him in the eye; the blinding sun is at his back, making it nearly impossible to make out his expressions.

"Touching what's mine."

"Do you mean *me*?" I reply, shocked by the possessive statement that just fell from his lips.

His head moves up and down slowly, nodding. "You're here to be my girl... not to be his plaything. I'll make it clear to him."

I'm confused. So, *so* confused. This is the most he's said to me in two days, and he's *so* close. The planes of his chest are right in front of me, so near I could press my palms against him and fill the space between our bodies. I can smell him too, masculine and woodsy. *Addictive.*

My head is swimming with confusion, swimming with *him.*

"I didn't mind. He was just being friendly," I say, my tone breathy.

He laughs humourlessly. "Well he can be friendly with someone else's girl."

He turns on his heel and moves swiftly back inside, and I'm left reeling, even more conflicted than I was before.

Josh might be magnetising, but Masen is all-consuming.

I don't know what just happened, but things just got a hell of a lot less boring, that's for sure.

***

"C'mon, FG, let's go see what he's been working on."

Josh grabs my hand and pulls me to my feet, dragging me along behind him towards the door that leads down to the basement.

Masen scowls at our joined hands – it appears that Josh didn't receive the message as loud and clear as I'm betting Masen would have delivered it.

At least I had time to throw a dress over my bikini before he got his hands on me again.

"I'm not really in the mood for sharing," Masen drawls.

"Well bad luck, sunshine, we're going down to the studio, no one said you had to come."

I pull my hand from Josh's and hide both behind my back so he can't grab either one again.

"I think I might just go up to my room..." I offer.

Masen looks relieved, but Josh is oblivious.

"Like fuck, you're coming with me," he states.

Masen steps in front of him, blocking his path.

"Oh quit being such a baby, if she's 'yours' when I try to kiss her, then she's *yours* now too, which means she gets to see everything."

My cheeks heat again as he confirms he was in fact intending to lock lips with me, and then redden further at the idea of being Masen's, even if it is just pretend.

Masen goes to open his mouth – probably to argue, but Josh cuts him off.

"I bet you had her sign some elaborate contract so she can't say shit anyway, so stop being a little bitch and let her in."

Masen lands his hand in the centre of Josh's chest, halting him.

"*Come on*, that thing will be so watertight, I bet I could piss in it and not lose a drop."

"Ew." I grimace. "That's disgusting."

Masen glances at me and then back to Josh before stepping aside with a heavy sigh and letting him past.

"Green light!" Josh yells to me as he rushes down the stairs. "Let's go, FG!"

I rub my temples. I've only known the guy an hour, and I'm already tired.

"Yeah... he has that effect," Masen grumbles as he starts to trail after his friend.

He turns back when I don't follow. "You coming?"

I shrug. "I don't have to."

He runs his hand through his hair, and as much as I don't want him to be uncomfortable, I'm dying for him to say yes, so I can check out his setup for myself.

"Oh, what the hell, you're going to be here a while, right? May as well get it over with."

I grin widely and rush down the steps after him.

I think he chuckles, but given that I've never heard him laugh, I wouldn't know if it was my imagination or not.

I follow him until we step into a huge room, all set up like a professional recording studio.

"*Wow*," I breathe.

This is like my dream come to life, and he hasn't even started singing yet.

Josh pats the chair next to him as he smiles at me. "Come sit."

I slowly cross the room, feeling Masen's eyes on me the entire time. "This is incredible."

My fingers trail lightly over the huge workstation while my eyes scour the recording booth.

He's got all kinds of instruments in here, a piano, drums, guitars...

"You play?" I tip my head towards the thousands of dollars' worth of equipment.

I've seen him live in concert once – not that he knows that – and he didn't touch an instrument, but that doesn't mean he can't play.

He shakes his head slowly, watching me intently.

It's clear he doesn't like people in his space all that much, but hey, I'm not particularly thrilled about the state of my life right now either, so it won't kill us both to be out of our comfort zones.

"He's lying, he can play," Josh drawls as he grabs hold of my hand and tugs me down so I'm sitting on the seat right next to him.

"You really don't know anything about personal boundaries, do you?" I ask him.

He grins wider, that sexy dimple of his appearing. "Oh, I'm aware they exist, I just prefer to ignore them. You'll get used to it." He taps the end of my nose.

I try but fail not to smile back at him. I don't know what it is about Josh, but he's so warm and inviting. He's the stark opposite to the other man in the room with us right now.

Masen is cold and unwelcoming. And confusing. Really, *really* confusing.

It scares me that even given that, I don't know whose company I'd choose if I had to pick just one.

As long as Josh doesn't try and kiss me again, I think I could get used to spending time with him quite easily, but Masen's time... I'm starting to crave it.

I tug my hand free from Josh's and turn so I can look at Masen, who is lingering awkwardly in the corner. "So, you *do* play?" I question.

He shrugs. "A little."

Jesus. Getting any form of conversation out of him is like getting blood out of a stone.

"Alright."

"Sing something already, I've got shit to do today." Josh crosses his legs at the ankles as he speaks, his arms splaying widely across the back of the seat.

"I'm not singing for you," Masen replies with a shake of his head.

"You sing for the world, don't be such a prick," Josh says, his grin growing.

Masen doesn't budge, doesn't even crack a smile.

"Fine then, I'll just find something on here." Josh leans forward, reaching for one of the hundreds of dials and buttons.

My hand darts out and catches his before he can touch anything. "Do you know how to use that?"

Josh chuckles. "Not a fucking clue, but I'm more than willing to push buttons until his eye twitches."

"I think you might have already succeeded," I reply dryly. "Maybe you should let me..." I tug his hand back and place it in his lap.

"You some kind of music-producing expert, FG?" He quirks a brow questioningly.

I shake my head. "I'm no expert, that's kinda why I'm doing the degree."

"You're studying music?" It's Masen who questions me this time, and much like every time he speaks directly to me, I feel his raspy voice all the way down to my toes.

I don't know how someone so young can have perfected being so intimidating. He's only twenty-three, yet he's got years and years' worth of life experience simply radiating from him.

I nod, my eyes not wandering from the elaborate setup in front of me. "Did you think I was running around getting coffees at the recording studio just for fun?"

I glance at him. He doesn't answer me, but his eyes study me with a look of curiosity.

I have to look away, his stare sees too much.

I slide one of the dials and press a few buttons. A beat fills the room.

I grin victoriously at the small win.

I spent a lot of time in a small recording studio back home, learning the basics every holiday break for the past three years, but the setup they had, had *nothing* on this. I don't even know what most of these gadgets do, but I'd kill to find out.

"Ten points to the new girl." Josh holds his knuckles out to bump against mine.

I fiddle with another few dials and then Masen's raspy voice fills the air, surprising me. I frown, glancing at the speaker, before realising that the voice is coming out of the man himself, not the recording equipment.

He sails through a verse of a song I've never heard before, and into the chorus, his voice belting out the chords effortlessly.

I fall back against my seat, transfixed by his beautiful face and voice as I get the show of a lifetime – one that half the women in the world could only dream about.

He stumbles through the next verse, before stopping all together. "It's a work in progress," he says with a shrug.

I twist a dial and the music dies down.

"Masen, that was *incredible*," I breathe.

His eyes rise from the floor to meet mine, the dark brown iris flecked with gold.

I swallow deeply. When he looks at me with that undiluted intensity, it's hard to remember that this is just business.

CHAPTER FIVE

Masen

"She's cool, man, I like her." Josh twirls a drumstick around his fingers.

I snatch it from his grasp and put it back where it goes.

I hate him being in my studio, he's so big and messy – he's always touching shit like a toddler.

He scowls at me, but it's short-lived, he's grinning again in no time.

"Have you checked out her ass? It's fucking fine."

"I'm not talking about her ass with you."

"So, you're telling me you haven't checked her out?"

I run my hand through my hair. "She's been living in my house all weekend. I've seen her. I've seen her skimpy bikinis and her tiny fucking shorts."

Jesus. Those tiny fucking shorts.

When I insisted that she live with me, I never anticipated that she'd look quite so sexy doing it.

She was meant to be sweet, not mouth-watering.

I'm not sure she owns any clothing that comes anywhere near her knees, but if she doesn't stop parading around wearing fucking *nothing*, I'm going to have to send her shopping.

I've hidden out in my studio for eighty percent of the weekend, just to try and get a reprieve from her floral scent wafting around the hallways, her sandals at the door, her book left lying on the kitchen counter... and don't even get me started on the second-floor bathroom.

I'm starting to wonder if this is all some elaborate prank set up by Chuck and Ange to pay me back for being such a prick all these years.

I thought choosing an innocent-looking young girl would make this easier, but I was wrong. So, so wrong.

"You want to screw her brains out, don't you?" Josh chuckles, his eyes locked on my face, reading my expressions in a way only he seems to be able to do.

Sometimes I wish I'd been *more* of an asshole rock star and cut off *everyone* I knew before I got famous – then I wouldn't have to deal with my childhood best friend turning up like he owns the place and throwing around his stupid opinions like he thinks I want to hear them.

"She's a teenager."

"Exactly." He waggles his brows at me. "Limber."

"You're a sick fuck."

"Whatever. It's not like she's underage."

I flip him off.

He laughs, almost doubling over. "Well, if you're going to let that sexy woman go to waste, I'll quite happily rifle through your trash can."

"Fuck off."

He crosses his arms across his chest, a knowing smirk plastered across his smug face. "You telling me she's *really* off limits?"

I know what he's doing. I've already warned him to keep his hands off Billie, but he's trying to goad me into confessing that I feel something I don't.

He wants me to admit that I want her for myself.

And I do. *Fuck*, I do, but it's purely physical... and I'm not willing to go there, not with her.

There are plenty of other sexy women out there to fill that void.

"If you fuck this up for me, I'll mess up that pretty face of yours."

He winks at me. "I just want to have some fun with her."

"Have your fun somewhere else."

He spins his chair, touching anything he can get his hands on as he goes around.

"Don't fuck this up. I could lose my record deal if this doesn't work. I'm not doing it for fun."

His chair stops spinning, and he looks at me, his expression grim. "That bad?"

I nod. "Yeah, it's that fucking bad. That's why she's here, I need her to help me clean up my public image, and if she's seen necking on with my best mate, that's going to look a little bit fucking suspicious, isn't it?"

He nods slowly, actually thinking before speaking for once.

"Fine," he grumbles. "But I'm still going to give her shit; I like it when she goes all red."

"Do whatever you want, as long as you keep your god damn hands to yourself."

He salutes me and I grind my teeth together.

Josh would probably do anything for me if it really came down to it, but that wouldn't stop him having the time of his life on the way.

"Where'd Billie go anyway?" he questions.

I shake my head. Fucked if I know. After I sang, she ditched, muttering something about washing her hair.

"I'm gonna go find her, see if I can make her blush some more."

He jumps to his feet and charges off out the door and up the steps, taking them two-at-a-time like the raging bull he is.

I drop into my chair and run my hand through my hair in frustration. I could really use a drink right about now.

Even just a sip would do it, but I know myself better than that. One sip is never enough, not for a guy like me.

I've always had an addictive personality, I get hooked on something, and I want more and more until I can't get enough.

Music was my first addiction, and that led to my second addiction – the booze. I even dabbled in drugs, but thankfully I didn't get a chance to get hooked.

That's the thing with drugs; you're high until you're not high anymore. Then you've only got two choices, get high again, or face the come down.

I could easily have fallen into that trap, and it was Josh of all people that put his foot down with me, got me out of that scene, away from that crowd and into rehab before it was too late.

He might be a giant fucking inconvenience most of the time, but I owe him for that. I owe him big time.

I hear a female shriek from upstairs, and I drag my hands over my face. Sounds like Josh found Billie.

***

Movement catches out of the corner of my eye, and I glance around.

Billie's head pops out from behind the doorframe. "Is he gone?" she asks, her tone hushed.

I turn back to the TV, so she won't see my grin.

"He left about half an hour ago," I tell her.

She sighs. "Oh, thank god, I mean he's a good guy, sexy as hell," she sighs, "but I'm *exhausted*. He's like a puppy you have to give constant attention to."

I find my jaw clenching without even consciously allowing the action.

She strolls into the room and drops her tight little body onto the couch next to me.

I hold back a groan; she's wearing a tiny pair of pyjama bottoms and a tank top that leaves nothing to the imagination – especially since she's clearly not wearing a bra.

Fuck.

I drag my eyes from her tits and force myself to stare at the movie on the screen.

"You think my best mate is 'sexy as hell'?" I question, glancing at her face only briefly, and not allowing my eyes to fall any lower.

She blushes. "Did I say that out loud?"

"Sure did."

She squirms around nervously.

"Well?" I prompt. I don't know why I'm pushing her, maybe I like that stain on her cheeks as much as Josh seems to.

"I mean, *yeah*... he's an attractive guy," she admits. "He's bright and bubbly... he's like the sun with his golden skin and his blonde hair. It's actually kinda blinding."

I huff out a breath.

If he's the sun, then I must be that point of darkness in the dead of the night.

"He's hasn't got that whole broody, musician thing going for him that you've got so down pat."

I turn my gaze on her, watching with interest as she fights to hold my stare rather than shy away from it.

"Do you think I'm sexy, sugar?" I ask her.

I watch as she swallows slowly – it seems to be a nervous habit of hers – the column of her throat moving in an alluring, seductive kind of way.

She goes to speak, but her words get caught on her lips.

She tries again, "I think you know *exactly* how sexy you are," she says, her voice husky.

I've seen entire websites dedicated to how 'sexy' I apparently am, but it's not something I think too much about. I am the way I am, and short of cleaning up my alcohol dependence, I'm not about to change a thing about myself.

I don't care about being sexy, but I have to admit, I like the sound of it when it comes from those lips.

She strokes her bright pink nails down her bare thigh, and I rise to my feet.

The urge to touch her, to *fuck* her, is only getting stronger, and I can't give in to it. Not with this woman anyway.

I haven't had sex with anything other than my hand since I checked into rehab three months ago, and it's taking its toll on my self-control.

I really need to get laid. Preferably by someone who *isn't* my fake girlfriend, and if I sit here much longer, that's exactly what's going to go down.

"I'm going to hit the hay," I tell her, avoiding her eye.

"Alright," she replies quietly. "Night."

I watch as she snags a throw rug off the back of the couch and tucks it around herself, like she's settling in for the long haul.

She turns her head, noticing that I've stopped in my tracks.

"Everything alright?" she questions.

Is everything alright? No. Fuck no. My life is a mess.

I nod. "See you tomorrow."

"Oh." She raises her finger. "I forgot to tell you, I have a full day of classes tomorrow, so I won't be around. I'll have my phone though... you know... if you need me or whatever."

My lip curls up in irritation, about what, I'm not sure.

"Fine."

Her eyes widen at the malice in my tone, but she doesn't say anything more, just turns back to the screen and keeps watching.

I stand there for a full minute longer, but if she knows I'm still there, she doesn't let on.

I finally slink out of the room, feeling oddly pissed.

"Morris," I bark as I enter the kitchen and see him wiping down the already-clean counter.

"Yes, Sir, what can I do for you?"

I've given up asking him to use my first name, he's been here two years now and I haven't succeeded yet.

"Billie will be going to her classes tomorrow; I want Eric to go with her."

Eric is the bodyguard I hired to keep an eye on her when she leaves the house – she's yet to meet him, so that should be interesting.

"Certainly, Sir. I'll have him ready and waiting by seven am."

I nod. "Good... Thanks."

"Not a problem."

I hover in the kitchen, and he eyes me curiously. "Was there something else?"

I nod, before glancing over my shoulder to make sure that Billie hasn't made her way into the room behind me.

"Have Eric keep his eyes and ears open. I want to know who her friends are, what classes she takes, if there are any guys sniffing around..."

"I'll instruct him to prepare a full report," he replies, not a hint of judgement in his tone.

I nod once, pissed with myself for my request, but unwilling to change my mind about it.

"Night," I grumble as I stalk from the room.

CHAPTER SIX

Billie

I tug Avery closer and loop my arm through hers, using her like a shield as we escape campus.

"I swear to god, if another stranger acts like my best friend again today, I'm going to lose my shit."

It's happened in *every* class, *and* at the recording studio when I called in there this week. Suddenly I'm a big deal now that I'm 'dating' the most untouchable man in music.

Avery giggles and waves to the few paparazzi who have stuck it out all week long.

I'm not sure what they think they're going to get a picture of me doing, but I can guarantee it's not going to be anything scandalous.

I'm the most boring rock star girlfriend in the history of the universe.

Eric holds open the door to the huge, tinted-out vehicle that I've been riding in every day since this fiasco started.

It's a far cry from the sleek, red convertible that I planned to drive myself to school in.

Letting me choose my car was a short-lived dream once we realised the magnitude of the press hounding me.

Masen bargained with me that if I let Eric chauffer me around in this tank of a vehicle, he'd let me drive the convertible up the coast to his holiday home this weekend *and* bring Avery with me.

He's barely spoken a word more to me in the past four days, so that was a deal I was all too willing to make.

I can't wait to escape his mood swings, and Josh with his sexy, impromptu visits.

I'm a walking ball of hormones, and I've never felt so out of control in my life.

I clamber into the car and Avery climbs in behind me.

She's coming to the house for the first time tonight and staying over so we can get an early start on the drive in the morning, neither of us have classes on Friday this week, so we thought we'd make a long weekend out of it.

Avery bounces in her seat as she takes in the plush interior of the no doubt ridiculously expensive car.

"Can you try and be cool?" I grumble.

She points a finger at me. "Don't you start. You're the least cool person I know."

I scowl at her. "Thanks."

She rolls her eyes. "You know what I mean, you have absolutely no chill. I bet you still stutter when Masen talks to you."

She's not far from the truth, but given that Masen barely speaks to me, it hasn't been that much of a problem.

"I'm more comfortable than I was."

"Wait until he takes you on the red carpet. You'll legit die."

"You *do* understand the meaning of the word 'legit', right?"

"You. Will. Die. RIP you." She giggles as we weave through traffic, Eric manoeuvring the huge vehicle with the skill of someone vastly overqualified to be babysitting me.

I shake my head at her.

She's going to embarrass me so thoroughly when we get home, *that* might actually kill me.

RIP me after all.

For a fleeting moment, I hope that Masen isn't there, that he's going to go and hide out somewhere for a long weekend too, but as quick as it enters my mind, it's gone again.

His presence intimidates me, but I crave it. He's like gravity, pulling me in while at the same time, doing his best to push me away.

"Do you think he'll sing for me?"

I try and fail to conceal a giggle as I think about how much effort it took on Josh's behalf to get me to be allowed into Masen's studio.

I don't think Avery has got a hope in hell, but I don't want to be the one to crush her dreams.

"What?" she demands.

I shake my head, my grin lingering. "I guess you can ask him."

She sighs dreamily, her strawberry-blonde curls bouncing as she wriggles in excitement.

We pull up outside Masen's place and Eric lowers his window to type his code into the gate, which promptly opens for us.

"Oh my god, this place is awesome," she squeaks.

One of the many garage doors opens, revealing a too-handsome-for-his-own-good man, his arms crossed tightly across his toned chest, his damp blond hair falling across his brow and a wide, easy grin on his lips.

"Who the fuck is that?" Avery demands, practically drooling.

I can't even blame her, he's delicious.

"Josh.," I breathe.

She shoves me. "Who the hell is Josh? Jesus, how many hot guys are you keeping in this place? Am I walking into some kind of orgy?"

I feel my cheeks heat as Eric catches my eye in the rear-view mirror. I'm pretty confident he's laughing, but I can't be sure.

Great.

She's managed to embarrass me even faster than I thought possible.

"He's Masen's best friend. He comes over a lot. And *no*, no orgies," I hiss.

Josh steps backwards, watching with interest as the car pulls into the garage in front of him.

"Why not? He's *hot*."

"Please stop talking," I beg as the car comes to a stop and my door swings open. A grinning Josh appears, his baby-blue eyes sparkling.

"Hey, FG, I missed you. What took you so long? Who's your friend?"

I can't help but smile, his excitement is infectious.

"I've been at class, some of us have better things to do than lounge around a pool all day, and this is Avery, she's staying over tonight."

His charming smile shifts from me to my best friend.

"Avery," he says simply, his voice husky.

I wince. I bet he's turned her to a puddle of mush with just that one word.

"Are you going to let us out of the car or what?" I demand.

He stares at Avery – who looks like she's forgotten how to speak – for a beat longer before chuckling and pulling his head back out of the car, gesturing for me to climb out.

"Wow," Avery whispers. "That was... wow."

I couldn't agree more. I still find myself thinking about the way he very nearly charmed the pants off me when we first met, not that he's any less appealing now, but he *is* more exhausting, that's for damn sure.

I slide out of the car, slinging my bag over my shoulder, and Avery follows.

"Thanks, Eric," I call to the man who's become my shadow.

He tips his invisible hat to me, the light bouncing off his bald head.

Josh shuts the car door, still making eyes at Avery. I shove him in the direction of the house, and he starts to walk, a chuckle falling from his lips.

"You didn't tell me your friend was so pretty, FG."

"I didn't tell you anything about my friend, in fact, I was hoping you wouldn't be here at all."

He clutches at his chest. "You wound me. It hurts my feelings when you're embarrassed of me, you know that?"

I roll my eyes and drop my bag onto a stool at the kitchen bench.

"Mi casa es su casa," Josh tells Avery, his hands gesturing around to the house.

I shake my head in amusement.

Avery glances around, her eyes wide. "This place is *amazing*."

Eric clears his throat from behind us. "Excuse me, Miss Tatum, what time are you planning to leave in the morning? I need to make the arrangements."

I narrow my eyes at him. "What kind of arrangements?"

"Notify the cleaning company of our arrival time, check our route, that type of thing."

My brows rise, nearly to my hairline. "I'm sorry, but *our*?"

He frowns at me in confusion. "Yes..."

"You think *you're* coming with us?" I demand.

"Of course," he replies as though it should have been obvious.

"Oh, uh thanks... but that won't be necessary." I hold up my hands in refusal. "We'll be fine on our own."

Eric's lips lift ever so slightly in the corners, it's the closest I've ever seen him come to smiling, even though I'm confident he's had a laugh or two at my expense behind closed doors.

"I'm sorry, Miss Tatum, but Mr. Lennox was *very* clear."

I grind my teeth together in frustration. I'm seriously considering stomping my foot right now.

"Are you going to ride in the back seat of the convertible?" I demand, my irritation obvious.

"Of course not. I'll follow you in another vehicle."

A string of words cross my mind, but I don't let any of them find their way out of my mouth.

"Thanks, but I'll pass. This is a girls' weekend."

Josh opens his mouth to say something, but he's cut off by a voice coming from the far corner of the room.

"You're not leaving this house without security, sugar."

I turn slowly until my eyes land on his.

Masen Lennox in all his glory.

I don't know how he makes a fitted black t-shirt and ripped jeans look so good, but there he is. Every sizzling inch of him.

I hear Avery gasp and Josh chuckle. "How long have you been standing there?" Josh asks.

"Long enough to hear you taking credit for my house."

Josh chuckles, his bare arm landing around my shoulders.

I shrug it off as I stare at the man who makes my heart race. He's leaning against the wall, his arms loosely crossed at his front, his biceps bulging against the sleeves of his tee.

"We had a deal," I say, my agitation growing. "I got chauffeured around all week like the freakin' queen for this."

He pushes off the wall, stalking towards me.

I swallow deeply, my resolve wavering. It's easier to stay strong with half a room between us.

"I agreed that you could drive the Ferrari up the coast this weekend, I never said *anything* about you going alone," he says as he comes to a stop in front of me.

I tilt my head up to meet his dark stare.

I frown as he reaches out, pressing the tip of his finger against the crease between my eyes.

"You won't know Eric's there," he promises, his hand falling to his side.

I scoff. "Oh yeah, he's really hard to miss."

The corner of Masen's lip twitches with amusement or irritation, I can't be sure which.

"It's final, sugar."

I set my hands on my hips defiantly. "We'll see about that."

His eyes narrow as he contemplates his next words.

"I'll make sure Oliver stays out of your way too," he says, his voice raspy and sexy.

I'm too busy thinking about the tingle running down my spine to register what he's said right away.

"Sorry, *what*? Why would Oliver be there?"

Oliver is Masen's bodyguard, so if Oliver is going to be there, then that means that...

"Because I'm going to be there." He finishes my thought for me.

Well fuck.

"Oh, sweet Jesus," I hear Avery whisper.

"Who's your friend, sugar?" Masen asks, his eyes never leaving mine.

"Avery," I whisper.

"Avery," he repeats, still not even so much as glancing at her.

"Hi," she squeaks.

I frown again, realising he's successfully distracted me. "Since when were you coming with us?" I demand.

"Since you decided to go," he replies simply.

I run my hand over my face and into my hair, the long strands tugging as I slide my fingers through.

"*Why?*" I ask warily.

Dear god, why?

I needed this weekend to escape. I needed some space to get my head on straight, but it doesn't seem like I'm going to get it.

He leans forward, his warm breath tickling my face as he whispers his reply. "Because I can, sugar."

I hear myself gasp as he tucks my hair back behind my ear.

"Pack your shit, Josh. We'll be leaving at eight am, Eric."

Masen steps back, Josh whoops with excitement, and Eric replies, "Certainly, Sir."

Eric holds a folder up in Masen's direction, and he takes it silently.

"Well shit," I mutter as I watch Masen stroll away, all swagger and sex appeal.

He doesn't look back once.

Josh grabs me, pulling me against his firm chest and swings me around. "Everything is more fun with you around, FG." He chuckles as he sets me back on my feet.

"You're ruining my girls' weekend," I grumble.

I want to argue, or make other plans, but I know it would be a waste of my time. Masen has decided something and that's how it'll be. This is his castle and he's the king.

"I'm *improving* your girls' weekend," Josh argues, gesturing to his body. "Just think of how much I'm enhancing the view."

"You're not wrong there," Avery replies.

I groan as Josh gives her one long, lingering look before jogging from the room in the direction Masen went.

"Well... this should be interesting."

CHAPTER SEVEN

Masen

I flick through the contents of the folder one more time before tossing it onto the desk and walking from the room.

Eric gave me everything I asked for. I know every subject she's studying, her professors' names, the name of every student she sits next to, and the names of every person that's spoken to her in the past week.

I'm not sure if she was this popular before she became my girlfriend, but she sure as fuck gets a lot of attention now, especially from males.

Not that I could blame anyone for looking twice, not when she's still rocking barely-there shorts every god damn day.

I blame those very shorts for my stupid decision to crash her girls' weekend.

That was never part of the plan, but when she stood there in my living room, her sassy attitude and her sexy legs cracked me.

I don't know who the fuck this chick thinks she is, trying to refuse security, but I wasn't having it. So now she's not only got *her* bodyguard coming, but me, Josh *and* my security too.

I smirk to myself as I think about the look on her face when she realised I was going to be there all weekend.

I intimidate her, I know I do. I know that she's attracted to me too. But she's also attracted to my best mate, and that pisses me off way more than it should.

It's probably going to make for a spectacular clusterfuck of a weekend if I had to guess.

I glance around the room once.

Morris has already taken my bag; it'll be in the back of the Range Rover by now. He might be too formal for my liking, but at least he's efficient.

As I stroll down the hall, I can hear Josh singing at the top of his lungs downstairs, and it's so fucking bad I can't even make out what song it is.

I hear Billie laugh and I pause, watching them with interest as they come into view.

My girl is sitting up on the bench, her wild hair in waves around her shoulders. She's smiling wide and looking fucking incredible in a black dress.

Josh is sweeping Avery off her feet, quite literally dancing her around my kitchen as he destroys the song he's still trying to sing.

They look so relaxed, so normal.

I should go back upstairs, make an excuse and leave them to a fun weekend without me ruining what should be a good time, but when Billie's hazel eyes find mine, I'm too selfish to walk away.

I step the rest of the way down, paying no attention to anything but the woman that the world thinks belongs to me.

Her cheeks pink and her tongue darts out to moisten her bottom lip as she watches me approach.

I should run in the opposite direction, but I can't seem to do anything but move towards her.

Josh bumps into me and Avery mutters an apology, but I don't even so much as glance at them.

"*Hi*," Billie whispers as I stop right in front of her.

Her legs fall open and I step even closer, so I'm between her thighs. Her breath hitches and I almost grin.

I haven't let myself get this close to her, but my control is waning, as is my desire to give a fuck.

She's too tempting.

The zip of my jeans presses against the bench top as my hands land on the cool surface on either side of her hips.

"Hi," I reply, my eyes grazing over every detail of her face.

Josh is still murdering Ed Sheeran's '*Castle on the Hill*', as I now recognise it to be, behind me, but Billie doesn't seem to notice that our friends are even in the room.

"Are you ready to go?" she asks, her voice shaky.

I let my gaze wander lower, ignoring her small talk.

"You look sexy as hell in this dress, sugar."

I watch her throat move as she tries to settle her nerves.

"Thank you," she finally whispers as I take my fill of her, right down to her bare feet.

Her toenails are painted the same pink as her fingernails and, I don't know why, but it only makes her more appealing.

I should back away, but I can't seem to make myself.

"So... you're driving?" I question as her eyes pull me back to her face.

She nods slowly. "If you trust me driving that expensive car?" she replies softly.

I couldn't give a fuck about the price tag. It's just money.

"You know how to drive, sugar?" I question as I lean in a fraction closer, the sweet scent of her filling my nose.

I inhale deeply and watch her shudder, a trail of goosebumps pebbling her exposed skin.

"Mmm hmm," she murmurs.

Her hand lifts from her lap and she reaches for me bravely.

I glance down, watching as she rests her palm against my chest, right over my rapidly beating heart.

My own hand reaches up, and I clasp her chin between my thumb and forefinger.

I lean closer and her eyes flutter closed.

I pull away just as our lips brush against one another, straightening up and stepping away, taking the zing of electricity with me.

Shit.

Her hand falls back to her lap as her eyes snap open.

She watches me curiously, the hurt I expected to see in her eyes absent, instead all I see is desire.

"We should go," I say.

"Shot gun," Josh yells, and it hits me that he and Avery are still in the room, probably watching everything that's just happened.

I turn away from Billie and head towards the garage with purpose in my stride. I need to get some space from her – clear my head... but I don't know how the fuck I'm planning to do that when I'm about to spend an entire weekend in her presence.

"You can't call shot gun if you can't see the car," Avery protests.

I hear Josh start to run up behind me and I hold out an arm to stop him. "If you think I'm sitting anywhere but in the front of my car, you're fucking high."

"Asshole," he grumbles.

I smirk with my back to him.

I get into the bright red car and nod to Eric and Oliver, letting them know we're ready to hit the road.

I feel Billie slip in next to me, but I can't look at her right now – not behind the wheel of my car, not looking like that.

I tug my sunglasses from my head to cover my eyes as the engine purrs to life.

This is going to be a long fucking weekend.

***

I glance over at her again, her hair whipping around her face, and that god damn dress riding higher up her thighs from the wind.

She gave up on the driving after about an hour and handed over the reins to me – *thank fuck*. The only thing hotter than a beautiful girl in your ride, is when she's behind the wheel or got her head in your lap.

Music is blasting from the stereo and it's a perfect result for me – it means there's no time for talking.

I glance in the rear-view mirror at Josh and Avery, who have gotten closer and closer over the trip. They're sitting as near to one another as humanly possible, and Josh is clasping one of Avery's legs in his lap, her body twisted in her seat to face him as she giggles and speaks into his ear.

He catches my eye and grins.

Fucking smug bastard.

My eyes roam lazily over the blonde that is bound to wind up in his bed before the weekend's out – she's pretty... hot body, but she's got nothing on Billie.

I shake the unwanted thought from my head.

I *really* need to get laid.

I just need to find a sexy, willing participant and screw her brains out so I can stop thinking about the woman I'm paying to be my girl.

I feel something touch my arm and my eyes snap back at Billie, and hell, her soft fingers are on my skin.

She waits until I'm looking at her face and then holds up her hands in a 'T'.

I huff out a laugh, my lips curling up into a small smile that I hope she doesn't notice. I'm not exactly known for smiling.

She grins and points to a sign stating that there are restrooms up ahead.

I tip my chin in response.

I see the rest area and ease the speeding car off the road, slowing down to stop for her.

Oliver and Eric are in the SUV behind us, and I see them indicate to follow us in.

I pull up to the side of the building and kill the engine, the blaring music cutting off with it.

"I *really* have to pee!" Billie cries as she rushes from the car in the direction of the toilet block. Avery leaps out after her.

Eric flies out of his vehicle, going to follow them, but I wave him off. "They're good," I yell after him.

We've been on the road for a long time now, we weren't followed, and no one around here is going to be looking for me or my girlfriend. We're in the middle of nowhere. That's why I love this place so much. The nearest town is a twenty-minute drive from my holiday house.

Eric nods warily and retreats back to his vehicle.

Poor bastard, I've never seen him move so fast. Maybe I've been a bit dramatic with the demands when it comes to Billie.

Josh leans through the middle of the front seats, his ever-present grin beaming at me. "So, I know you said FG was off limits, but her friend is fair game, right?"

I let my head fall back against the seat. "As long as you're not touching Billie, I don't give a fuck who you're doing what with."

He fist-pumps the air, and I try not to let his enthusiasm rub off on me.

"You know what I think?" he says just when I'm appreciating the silence.

I shake my head, lowering my glasses down my nose to get a better look at the toilet block the girls still haven't emerged from.

"I couldn't even imagine," I drawl as I push the dark lenses back into place, frowning.

"I think you like her."

"*Who*?"

"Billie. You like her."

"I don't dislike her."

He shoves my shoulder. "Bro, you know what I mean."

"Do I?" I ask tightly.

"She gets your dick hard. Try and deny it."

She gets my dick *real* hard, but I'm not about to tell him that.

"I haven't had sex in three months, my dick is always hard."

"You should take care of that."

"Plan to," I mutter.

I glance at the door again, but there's still no sign of the girls. "What the fuck is taking them so long?" I demand.

He shrugs. "They're chicks, man, I'm not going to pretend I understand what they do when they go into a bathroom together."

"I'm going to go find out." I reach for the handle of my door so I can go and see what's taking so long, but Josh's hand lands heavily on my shoulder.

"They're females, give it another couple of minutes. Trust me."

I drop my hand and reluctantly nod.

I watch two more minutes tick over on the clock and I'm just about to go and see if Billie is alright when the door opens and the two of them appear, giggling about something.

I relax back into my seat.

"Try telling me again how you're not into that girl, man, just try me," Josh says as I start the engine, so I can drown out his words.

Stupid smug bastard couldn't be more wrong.

CHAPTER EIGHT

Billie

"This is some beach house," I breathe as I turn in a slow circle, taking in the mansion before me.

I was expecting something small, cute... not *this*.

"It's sick, right?" Josh drawls, his grin somehow wider than it was when we pulled in.

I roll my eyes. "I wasn't talking to you, Joshy, this isn't your house."

He scowls. "I'm going to pretend you didn't just call me Joshy."

"You can pretend all you like, it won't make it any less true." I smirk as I slide open the huge glass doors that lead out to an unbelievable view of the beach.

There's a pool, a fire pit... everything you could ask for.

"I can feel my dick shrinking just thinking about that pansy nickname." He shudders as I turn back around to face him.

"Could be worse, I could have gone with Joshikins."

I can't help it, the look on his face is one of pure horror. I'm still laughing when Avery comes back into the room.

"I think the downstairs bathroom is bigger than our whole apartment," she hisses, eyes wide.

"You should see the cinema," Josh says, his torment over his penis forgotten the minute she entered the room.

"*Cinema*?" Avery demands.

"It's just a fucking media room; I'm not that much of a tool." Masen's voice comes from the doorway and my eyes instinctively follow the sound until I'm looking right at him.

His dark eyes are staring right at me, like gravity pulled them there.

Breathing is easier and more difficult at the same time.

"Eric and Oliver gave the all clear."

I nod my head, as though having security do a sweep of the property is something normal that happens in my everyday life.

"Sweeeet." Josh drags out the middle of the word as he tugs the t-shirt he's wearing over his head.

He flashes a panty-dropping smile at poor Avery, and I watch as her jaw drops open in shock at the sight of his chiselled, golden torso.

Been there, sweetie, been there.

He charges off, out through the door I left open and two seconds later, we hear the splash of him hitting the water of the pool.

"Sweet baby Jesus," Avery whispers, her eyes still trained on the space he last occupied.

"Yip." I nod in agreement.

"Did you see all his abs? Are there meant to be that many?"

I giggle. "If you play your cards right, he'll probably let you touch them."

"Screw touching, I want to lick melted chocolate off them." She sighs.

I hear a chuckle and look up in surprise. I've never heard Masen laugh. The warm, throaty sound is like music to my ears.

"Masen Lennox, did you just laugh?" I demand.

There's no sign of a smile on his face, but I see it in his brown eyes, he can't fool me anymore.

"What do you think, sugar?" he drawls.

I step towards him at the same moment that Josh yells out, "Avery, baby, get that sexy ass out here."

Avery doesn't need to be told twice, she's tugging her dress off, revealing her bikini in a flash and taking off after him.

I shake my head in amusement.

Those two are so getting it on.

"Your friend better be good about using protection, because Avery is terrible at taking her pill, and the last thing anyone needs is little mini Joshs running around."

I haven't built up the courage to look back at Masen now that we're alone, but I see him moving out of the corner of my eye, coming in my direction.

He comes up behind me, ignoring my warning. The curve of my lips fall, and my breath comes out in heavy pants.

I feel his fingers graze ever so softly up my arm and down my collar bone.

He sweeps the thick mass of hair from my shoulder and drops it so it trails down my back.

"Did you pack your sexy bikinis, sugar?" he asks, his deep voice right at my ear.

A shudder rocks my body, and I swear I can feel him smiling at the reaction he's just created.

I nod my head slowly, my eyes trained on the horizon line.

"You gonna wear one for me?"

I bite down on my bottom lip to keep from moaning and nod my head again.

"What about those short shorts? You gonna tease me with those too?"

His fingers find my skin again, this time running from my shoulder up to my neck.

I can't hold back my whimper of appreciation this time, instead tipping my head away from him to allow him better access.

"Hmm, sugar?" he prompts.

"*Yes*," I whisper.

"Good," he replies huskily, the one simple word nearly turning me to jelly.

His lips brush my shoulder and my lids flutter closed. By the time I open them again, he's gone.

I stand there, committing to memory how his lips felt on my skin.

"You look like you're about to orgasm, FG."

I wish.

I glance behind Josh, but there's no sign of Avery yet, so I pin him with my best 'I mean business stare'.

"Uh oh." He winces. "What the hell is that look for?"

"I'm just going to say this once and then we never speak of it again."

"Okay."

"You put your dick near my best friend, you wrap it, got it?"

His expression slowly morphs from shock to shit-eating grin. "You worried about me knocking up your friend, FG?"

"Little bit if I'm honest." I set my hands on my hips.

He flicks his wet hair, sending a spray of water flying across the room before taking steps towards me, all smokin' hot muscles and gorgeous blue eyes.

I swear he could probably get a girl pregnant with just that look alone.

I swallow deeply, my nerves coming to the surface. I might be all kinds of hung-up on Masen, but I'm not blind. Josh is sexy as hell. That level of hot can't go unnoticed.

"You know what, FG? I think you've got better things to worry about," he whispers as he leans in towards my ear.

"Like what?" I reply, my voice shaky.

"Like the fact that my boy is having a hard time convincing himself to keep his hands off you."

I huff out a laugh. "Bullshit."

He winks at me before strolling away, leaving my mind reeling, from his abs or his words, I'm not entirely sure.

"I'm telling you, FG, he's got it bad," he yells over his shoulder.

I don't believe him for a second, but it doesn't change the fact that I'm longing for Masen to touch me again already.

"Shit," I mutter.

Nothing good can come from any of this.

***

"I'm picking the movie!" Avery yells as she hauls ass into the media room, and I have to admit, Josh wasn't really wrong – this thing is huge.

A massive big-screen on one wall and the comfiest-looking couches staggered on two platform levels.

It's just like a cinema, but even better because it comes complete with two of the hottest guys I've ever laid eyes on.

I'm all for candy with my movie, but this is candy that's just for my eyes, and it's ridiculously good.

Josh bounds to the back couch and throws his body down along it. "Avery, baby, come sit with me."

Her eyes light up and she rushes after him, pausing when he doesn't move his legs for her to sit down, instead he chuckles, wraps his long arm around her middle and drags her down, so she's lying, the little spoon to his big.

They're cute together. If Josh wasn't a player and Avery wasn't a fruit loop, they could have something special.

"Looks like you're with me, sugar," Masen rasps, and my insides quiver. The way he calls me 'sugar' makes me weak in the knees.

I've sat with him before, but not in the dark, surrounded by what I assume is soon to be a make-out session by our best friends. I feel like a teenager on her first movie date all over again, only I doubt that Masen is going to yawn and subtly put his arm around my shoulders or cop a feel of my boob.

He points to the couch, and I pick a side, sinking into the plush fabric.

I moan in appreciation. "Oh. My. God. This feels so good."

"No need to imagine what you would sound like in the bedroom, huh, FG?" Josh chuckles, and I feel myself blush bright red.

I see Masen move, quick as a cat, and a cushion flies back, smacking Josh right in the face.

"Ow." He huffs, tossing it back. "What the hell was that for?"

"I told you not to touch my girl," Masen replies lazily, and my focus snaps back to him.

"I didn't touch her!"

"Maybe not in real life," Masen mutters, and Josh throws a hand up in outrage.

"So now you're going dark on me because I *imagined* her having an orgasm?"

I cover my face with my hands, blushing even though this entire conversation is based on nothing but Josh's dirty mind. "Can we please stop talking about this?"

"*Please*," Avery agrees. "You all need to shush, I'm putting the movie on."

I settle deeper into the couch, my face still flaming as the opening credits start to roll across the huge screen.

Masen pulls out his phone and taps away for a few seconds, then we're enveloped in darkness, just as I feared we would be.

It's the weirdest thing, I can barely even see him, but I'm hyper aware of every move he makes, as though I can sense him there, only a few feet away.

I need to get a hold of myself. I don't know what it is about him, but he's taking up far too much real estate in my brain.

It's unhealthy. I'm obsessed with everything about him.

The title of the movie comes across the screen and Josh groans loudly. "Really, baby? *The Notebook*? Are you trying to kill me?"

"It's a classic," Avery replies.

"It's a chick flick. Can't we watch *Thor* or something?"

"As much as I love me some Chris Hemsworth, my decision is final. Any and all complaints must be made in writing and sent to 'I don't give a fuck, at twenty-four, Get-over-it Lane'. Mmmkay?"

"I'll give you a fuck you'll care about," Josh retorts.

I groan. They've got each other started now.

"Shut the fuck up. If I've got to watch this shit, I at least want to hear it," Masen grumbles.

They banter back and forth in whispers for a few minutes and then I swear I can hear them kissing.

I bite down on my bottom lip to keep from laughing.

"Un-fucking-believable," Masen mutters.

I don't know what the hell happened to my life, but if someone had told me a year ago that I'd be here, watching a romantic movie with one of the biggest superstars on the planet, I would have laughed and told them they were crazy.

I shake my head in amusement and disbelief.

"What's so funny, sugar?" Masen whispers, shifting himself closer to me as he asks.

I suck in a breath, I didn't know he was watching me.

"I thought you wanted to watch the movie."

The screen lightens, throwing a dull glow over us and I'm struck again by just how freaking gorgeous he is.

"I don't give a shit about the movie."

"It's a great love story," I whisper, pointing at the screen, trying to get his intense stare to shift from me, but it doesn't work. His eyes don't budge from mine.

"It's total bullshit," he replies gruffly.

"What is?"

"*Love*. All this one-true-love crap."

I frown at the sincerity in his tone.

"You don't really believe that, do you?"

His dark eyes trail over my face slowly, taking in every inch before he answers. "I could ask you the same question."

I huff out a breath. *Of course* I believe in love.

Love is *everything*.

I want true love.

I want my very own prince charming.

I want my happily ever after.

He searches my expressions one more time, then wordlessly turns back to the movie like he didn't just confess to thinking true love is a joke.

CHAPTER NINE

"It's hot as balls out here." Avery moans as she shifts a little to her left, trying to stay in the shade of the umbrella.

"Get in the pool, babe," Josh replies, "*Or* we could go inside and I'll show you how hot *my* balls are?"

I roll my eyes behind my shades.

I don't know how the fuck the guy gets so many chicks with lame-ass lines like that, but they just fall at his feet. Over and over and over again.

I once saw him pick up a chick with nothing more than a beckon of his finger.

That was it. Putty in his god damn hands. Didn't even speak a word to her.

I mean, shit, I might not say much, but that's a joke.

My gaze slides to Billie for the one hundredth time, and it's as if she can feel my eyes on her, because she sits up, her perky fucking tits bouncing in her barely-there bikini as she looks at me.

"I'm going swimming, who's coming?"

She stretches her arms high above her head, and no fucking way am I going near that, not unless she wants to be stripped bare and taken right here next to the pool.

I need to keep my god damn distance – that's what I need to do.

"I think I know someone who *wishes* he was coming," Josh drawls, his shit-eating grin pointed right at me.

I flip him off, adjust myself in my shorts and grab my pack of smokes.

"You know, they say kissing a smoker is like licking an ash tray," Billie says, and I halt the cigarette in the air, mid-way to my lips.

I smirk. "You asking to test that theory, sugar?"

Her eyes widen, her smart-ass grin sliding off her face.

She stands up, the towel around her waist falling to the ground, and she's all long, bare legs and sexy mussed-up hair.

Fuck.

I am so fucked. She's a walking wet dream.

"It's a dirty habit, that's all I'm saying." She holds her hands up in defence as she strolls towards the edge of the pool.

"Yeah, man, it's a dirty habit," Josh parrots, trying his best to rile me up.

"Why don't you fuck off inside?"

He blows me a kiss, and I resist the urge to smack him.

I light my cigarette and take a long drag as I watch Billie raise her hands above her head and dive gracefully into the water, popping up a moment later.

She swims to the side of the pool, while I pretend not to watch with rapt attention, and lifts her arms to the edge, so she's perched there.

I nearly choke on my smoke.

The only thing sexier than Billie in a bikini, is her in one soaking wet.

"You coming in?" she asks me, a devious smirk on her lips.

She might scream sweet and innocent, but right now, I'm god damn certain she knows exactly what she's doing.

I shake my head, not trusting myself to say a word.

"Why not?"

Why not?

Isn't that just a loaded little question...

It's not that I don't want to get in that pool, but I know damn well if I start taking my clothes off and getting up close and personal with this girl, then it won't be close enough. That tiny scrap of fabric covering her won't last half a second, and the things I want to do to her aren't fit for public consumption.

That's fucking *why not.*

"He doesn't trust himself around you when you're so moist, FG," Josh answers for me.

Sweet fucking Christ.

Billie shoots him a look of disbelief and Avery pretends to gag.

"That's *disgusting.*"

"Doesn't make it any less true though does it?" He grins back.

"Don't *ever* let me hear you say the word 'moist' again," Billie demands.

The asshole winks at her. "I'm going to get it printed on a t-shirt, just for you. Mooooiiissst." He gestures across his chest.

"Yeah well you can shove that t-shirt right up your –"

"Enough," I bark, rising from my seat and stalking off down the beach.

The last thing I need is to be thinking about *that* girl, *this* way.

She might be here to help me out, but right now it feels like someone sent her to trap me in my own personal hell.

She's like a bottle of whiskey to me – no matter how much I want to down the whole thing in one go, I'm not even allowed a little taste.

I drag my cell from my pocket as I put as much distance between myself and the house as possible.

"What's going on?" Chuck answers.

"Nothing," I reply.

"Why'd you ring me then?"

I shrug, not answering. I don't fucking know why I called.

"You got a problem up there?" he tries again.

Yeah, I've got a problem, a real big fucking problem and it's standing at attention in my shorts, but I doubt Chuck wants to hear about that.

"Ange been off your case since Billie moved in?" I question.

He pauses for a moment, no doubt sensing that I didn't call to make small talk.

"Nah, she's been a raging bitch, but if you tell her I said that, I'll ruin you."

I smirk, trying not to chuckle. Pretty sure I've got ruining me covered all on my own.

"Whatever, man. Tell her it's under control. The press are eating Billie and me up. The cameras love her."

"And what about you, how are you dealing with having a chick at your place?"

I glance back down the beach towards the house, and I see her, sitting on the fence, watching me.

She waves at me and, like an idiot, I raise my hand and wave back.

"Masen?" he questions.

"Yeah... fuck, it's alright. I dunno... could be worse."

I drag my gaze from Billie and walk even further down the beach. It's a waste of my time. I couldn't escape her if I tried. If she's not in my sight, she's right there in my mind.

"Just keep it in your pants and we'll be golden," he reminds me.

I'm all too aware of the fact that it's in my pants and absolutely nowhere else.

"Yeah, yeah."

"Gotta go, kid, good chat."

I huff out a humourless laugh. "Yeah."

"Maybe next time you call me, you'll actually say what you called to say."

I hang up the phone. Maybe, but I doubt it.

***

"Where'd the love birds go?" I question Billie as I find her alone in the kitchen, cutting up a carrot.

She pops a piece in her mouth and shrugs.

"Are they still here?"

"Dunno."

"Where's Eric?"

She shrugs again.

I narrow my eyes at her. I don't know what the fuck I've done to deserve the silent treatment. I don't know why I care either.

"You pissed at me, sugar?"

Her breath hitches at the use of her nickname, and my lips twitch in amusement.

I love the way she reacts to me. It's hot as hell.

She catches herself staring and looks away, still munching on her god damn carrot.

"I'm not pissed at you," she says, going back to her chopping.

"Still trying to figure out if I taste like an ashtray?"

Her hands pause, then resume the action.

"Nope."

I scowl at the back of her head.

I'm a fucker for being irritated. This is the treatment she's received from me ever since she arrived, and here I am – getting it back for thirty seconds and I can't take it.

Maybe that's her game.

Well I can play games too.

I snag a piece of carrot from her chopping board and brush past her, my front pressing against her back for the briefest of seconds, but the joke's on me. Her floral scent hits me like a wrecking ball, assaulting my senses and making me crave her. I could drown myself in her perfume and I'd still want more.

I cross the room quickly, trying to clear my head, but I swear the scent comes with me, clinging to me – *torturing* me.

My phone dings and it's a text from Josh, telling me that he's taken Avery out for dinner. Eric's playing chauffer. Lucky him.

"Looks like it's just me and you tonight, sugar."

Her eyes meet mine and widen. "Where's Avery?"

"Being subjected to a date with Josh."

Her eyes soften and a smile curves up at her lips. "I think he likes her."

I think he just likes the idea of getting into her pants, but I'm not about to be the prick that says it out loud.

"He took her out for dinner?"

I nod.

"That's so sweet."

Like fuck it is. Josh isn't sweet.

I don't reply.

"Imagine if they got married and had babies one day – the story they'd have to tell of how they met through us."

Us. The word bounces around inside me, trying to force its way in deep.

There is no us. There never will be.

She sighs, her expression dreamy, and goes back to whatever the hell she's cutting up now.

"You want to go on a date, sugar?" The words are out of my mouth before I can consider the weight they carry – the implication of them if she were to say yes.

She laughs, a nervous giggle. "With *you*?"

I nod. Jesus. Someone hand me a fucking shovel, I'm digging myself a deep hole here.

"That's okay. You don't have to take me out."

I breathe a sigh of relief, thanking God that I don't have to take her to some fancy restaurant and pretend when all I really want to do is stay here and see the real her.

"What about takeout?" I offer. "I'll get you anything you want."

"Yeah?"

"*Anything.*"

She nods, thoughtful. "Alright, Masen Lennox, you got yourself a date."

CHAPTER TEN

Billie

I'm expecting a TV dinner, so when he sets up our takeout at the dining table, positioned so that we're facing each other, I'm surprised.

He's been distant, aloof, cold even towards me for the past day or so, and I can't get a read on him.

He seems to want me close, but not too close.

Sometimes it's like he really couldn't give a flying fuck about me, barely even glancing in my direction, but then he does something like chew Josh out for even thinking about me in the bedroom, and I'm right back to having absolutely no clue where I stand with him.

Like right now, as the guy I've crushed on for years sits across from me, holding out a set of chopsticks for me to take like it's no big deal at all that we're on a sort-of date.

We eat in silence, our only interaction when he leans across the table and steals a piece of chicken from my bowl and I try to smack him with my chopsticks.

I figure this is how the entire evening is going to go, so when he looks at me all dark eyes and smouldering looks and asks about my family, I'm shocked.

"You got any sisters, sugar?"

I shake my head. "N... no. No sisters."

Great. We're back to stuttering now.

One corner of his mouth lifts, my discomfort clearly amuses him. *Asshole.*

I drop my chopsticks, too on edge now to eat anymore. "Are you not going to ask if I have any brothers?"

He huffs out a humourless laugh. "I already know you haven't got any of those."

"How?" I ask, confirming that he is in fact correct with that one word.

"No one has threatened to kick my ass since we got together," he explains.

"What if I had a younger, nerdy little brother or something? One that doesn't know how to punch?"

He shakes his head, cocky in his assumptions. "Nope. No brother, no matter how nerdy, would watch his sister date a guy like me and not say a word."

My eyes roam over him. "Are *you* someone's brother?"

"Not that I'm aware of," he mutters under his breath.

I want to know what he means by that, but he's clearly not in the mood for sharing, he's in the mood for asking.

"What about your olds?"

I nod. "My mum and dad. They still live in the same house I grew up in. Doing the same jobs... still got the same friends."

"What do they think about you getting mixed up in my life?"

I lift one shoulder. "They're good people. I told them I knew what I was doing, and they asked when I was bringing you home for a Sunday roast."

"They invited me for dinner?" he questions, surprised.

I nod. "Yeah."

"You didn't tell me."

I snort. "No, I *didn't*. It's not like we're going to go home and have dinner with my parents."

"What if I wanted to?"

"You don't."

"You don't know that. You didn't ask."

I roll my eyes. "Fine. My parents invited us for dinner, do you want to go?"

"Fuck no," he says, a grin spreading across his handsome face. "Do I look like the kinda guy you take home to your folks?"

I lose it.

"You're such a dickhead," I say between giggles.

He laughs, his grin still in place, and it steals the breath right out of my lungs.

He's too much. I can't handle a guy like him.

Our laughter dies off and is replaced by a longing stare on my behalf and the usual intense focus from him.

"You want to produce music?" he asks when I'm about to spontaneously combust.

I can't take much more of this, my nerves are shot, my lips are aching for him and the air between us is practically crackling.

"I'd love to work with music in any way," I reply, grateful for the distraction.

"Do you like my music, sugar?"

I nod, embarrassed to admit I'm a complete and utter fan girl. I'm sure I told him something of the sort when we first met, but he's never called me on it. Until now it would seem.

"You shake that sexy ass when you sing along to my songs?"

My cheeks heat.

I'll never get over hearing him call me sexy. *Never.*

"If I told you that, I'd have to kill you."

He smirks.

"What about you? What music do you like?"

"Anything," he replies quickly. "I'll listen to anything."

"I didn't ask what you listen to, I asked what you like. There's a difference."

His lip twitches and he nods.

"Fair. I like older stuff. Fleetwood Mac, The Beatles, Elvis..."

He'll be one of those names one day.

"I approve."

He lifts his brows. "I'm glad," he drawls, his tone making it clear that he really couldn't give two shits about having mine or anybody else's approval.

I think that's what I admire the most about him – he's not looking for anyone's validation. That, and his insane talent.

Sure, he wants to fix his public profile, but that's for *him* – to get what he wants – keep his recording contract so he can keep doing what *he* wants to do.

"What are you always reading?"

"Books?" I answer, confused by his question.

"What kind of books?"

I nibble on my bottom lips, feeling oddly embarrassed to tell him. "Romance mostly."

He lifts a brow. "Like porn?"

I snort out a laugh. "No, not like porn. If I wanted to read nothing but sex, I'd just watch the real thing."

"You watch porn, sugar?" he asks with a smirk.

"Not nearly often enough," I tease.

"Do you –"

"Don't I get a turn asking the questions?" I interrupt him.

He scowls, but waves for me to go ahead.

Shit. I didn't expect him to give in so easily, I don't even know what I want to ask him.

"Wha... what's your favourite colour?"

"Black."

I'm surprised he doesn't add 'like my soul' to the statement, given the darkness of his expression, but I won't let it deter me.

"Tell me about the drinking."

He narrows his eyes. "Nothing to tell. I'm sure you saw it all in the press anyway."

"Tell me about rehab then."

"Wasn't my favourite place."

I plead with my eyes, begging him to give me something, *anything* real.

"It was the best and the worst thirty days of my life," he murmurs. "It was the first time I've looked in the mirror and hated what I'd become."

I swallow deeply, well aware that this is more of an insight to the real him than I've ever got before.

He shifts in his seat, and I can see I'm losing him.

"Do you have any tattoos?" I ask, trying to hold onto whatever we have going right here and now.

He shakes his head. "None."

"That's not very rock and roll of you."

"Don't like needles," he replies, and I'm freaking pathetic, because knowing that tiny little snippet of information about him, thrills me.

My face must show just how happy I am, because he pushes out of his seat, rounding the table as he says, "I think that's enough Q and A for one night."

I nod, disappointed and ridiculously satisfied at the same time, as he leans down towards me.

"Sweet dreams, sugar." His lips brush the lobe of my ear, and I shudder.

I wait until I'm sure he's gone before I get up from my seat, even more confused than when I sat down.

***

"I can't wear this," I hiss as I look at myself in the mirror.

We've been holed up in this beautiful house for the better part of two days, doing nothing but swimming, lounging around and eating – add in excessive amounts of flirting as far as Avery and Josh are concerned – but tonight, for our last night here, Josh has announced that we're going clubbing.

I didn't pack for clubbing.

Avery, however, *did*… and by 'packed for clubbing' I mean she brought a collection of her skankiest dresses and highest heels, because apparently you never know when you're going to need to dress like a hoe.

"You're wearing it. I'm going to get a different pair of shoes, wait here," she instructs as she rushes from my room.

I tug on the hem again, but it makes no difference, this thing barely covers my ass.

I can't let Masen see me wearing this. Not after he's already commented on how short my shorts are – this jumpsuit makes them look modest – and the way I keep feeling his eyes on my body whenever he's around is starting to feel dangerous.

Where Josh is openly flirty, it's Masen who holds my attention captive without any effort on his behalf.

Every stolen glance feels like foreplay, and every time he calls me 'sugar', I get weak in the knees.

It's stupid – crushing on him when there's no way he could be interested in someone as plain as me, but every now and then, there's a look in his eye that makes me think I could have a shot.

I tug the straps from my shoulders and slide the jumpsuit down my middle and over my ass as I let it drop to the floor.

I can't wear this. Not in public anyway.

I hear footsteps in the doorway and I turn, expecting Avery. "I'm not wearing..." The words die on my lips as I take in Masen; he's wearing dark jeans and a black button-down shirt, the collar open and the sleeves rolled up his forearms.

Fuck, he looks so good.

"*Jesus*, sugar." He groans.

It's only then that I realise I'm standing before him in nothing more than a strapless bra and a scrap of lace between my thighs.

"*Masen*," I whisper.

He looks at me like the one word pains him.

"I was just getting dressed."

I reach for the clothing at my feet, but his voice stops me. "*Don't.*"

I stand back up slowly, my hands empty.

He steps into the room and closes the door behind him. He's seen me in a bikini a hundred times, but this feels different, more intimate.

I can barely remember how to breathe as he stalks towards me, his greedy eyes taking his fill of my exposed body.

My heart is pounding in my chest. It's so loud I can hear it whooshing in my ears.

"Are you trying to kill me?" he growls as he reaches me, his hands landing on my hips and tugging me flush against him.

I shake my head. I can't speak. I wouldn't know what to say, where to begin.

His fingers skim lightly up my sides and a moan slips from between my lips.

"Fuck it," he whispers before he clasps my face in his hands and crashes his lips to mine roughly.

My hands find his chest and press against the hard plains.

He presses his tongue to the seam of my lips. I open to him and he frantically sinks into my mouth.

Holy shit, I was wrong. He tastes fantastic.

My fingers find the buttons on his shirt at the same moment that one of his hands finds the long hair trailing down my back.

He tugs, *hard*, pulling my head back, exposing my throat to him.

I moan again as he drops his mouth from mine and devours the skin at my neck.

I get the last button undone on his shirt and he's got it off in a flash.

I shove him back so I can look at him. I'm yet to see him without a shirt on, and *fuck* it was worth the wait. His abs are toned and tight and he's got the hottest 'v' I've ever seen in real life, with a tempting trail of dark hair leading into his waistband.

His eyes are dark and smouldering as they meet mine, and I shiver, a chill passing over me from the tip of my head down to the soles of my feet.

No guy has ever looked at me like this before.

He steps towards me and I reach for the belt around his hips greedily.

He groans, pained, and his head falls to my shoulder.

"I can't, sugar," he says, his voice strained.

"*What?*" I whisper, shocked by this sudden change of heart. "Why?"

My hands fall to my sides as he straightens, stepping away from me to put space between us.

"I can't do this, not with you."

I nod slowly, the reality hitting me like a slap across the face.

I don't know how I could be so stupid. I forgot who he is. He's not just *some guy*. He's Masen fucking Lennox, and he could *never* be mine.

"Of course... I... *sorry...*" I wrap my arms around my middle and step around him. "I shouldn't have... I mean, why would *you* want anything to do with *me?*" I laugh bitterly and snag the jumpsuit off the floor.

He doesn't reply as I quickly put it on, my back to him the entire time.

I don't allow myself to look back as I rush from the room.

CHAPTER ELEVEN

Masen

I know I've hurt her. I can see it plain as day. It's written all over her face.

I know I've said the wrong thing, that she's interpreted it the wrong way... but the wrong way is one hundred times safer than the right way at this point, so I let her redress in silence, and I don't say a word even as she rushes from the room without so much as a glance in my direction.

"Fuck," I mutter.

I've fucked this up good and proper.

I let my dick do the thinking and I can't allow that to happen when she's around.

She's not just some chick I can take to bed and disregard when I'm finished.

She'll still be here in the morning, and the morning after that, and the fucking one after that too.

She'll be here every morning until Ange decides my reputation is squeaky clean enough and, given the fucking attitude she gave me on the phone this morning, I'd say she's still far less than impressed.

"Fuck," I repeat as I grab my shirt off the floor and shrug it back on, fastening the buttons swiftly.

Putting it back on is nowhere near as exciting as taking it off was.

I don't know what the hell is going on with me, but I do know one thing, I'm a liability as far as Billie is concerned, even more so when I'm walking around with this loaded gun in my pants.

Jerking off doesn't even cut it anymore, I need the real thing.

I drop down and rest my head in my hands.

I haven't been this pissed off with myself since before I went into rehab.

"Tonight's gonna be a good night…" Josh bellows, murdering the Black Eyed Peas hit song and I groan in frustration.

I've got a matter of seconds before he finds me in here, sitting on the end of her bed looking like a chump, but I don't think I care enough to move away from the scene of the crime.

"Well, well, well, what do we have here? You look like you just got a blow job that was all teeth or something."

Jesus Christ. I need a smoke.

"Not in the mood for your shit, Josh."

"Well bad luck, princess, because here I am."

I lift my head slowly to look at him. He's gone all out, even styling his blond hair in something other than his usual 'I've just been surfing' style.

He leans against the door frame and crosses his arms across his chest.

"Where's FG?"

I shrug.

"You were a dick, weren't you?" he accuses, eyes narrowed.

I flip him off.

"What'd you do to her? Or did you finally bang her, and she was a dud in the sack?"

"*No*," I growl. "Shut the fuck up."

He smirks. "You're right, there's no way that girl is going to be a bad lay."

I can't listen to him talk about her while I sit on her unmade bed. It's too easy to imagine how she'd look naked beneath me, her dark hair against the white sheets.

Fuck.

I push to my feet and stalk past him.

"Grumpy fucker," he mutters.

He's not wrong, and he's also not doing a single damn thing to help my mood. As per fucking usual.

"Get the girls."

I see him salute me from the corner of my eye.

"Sir, yes, Sir."

***

The club is pumping around me, the heavy beat pulsing through the wall I'm leaning against.

I tug my ball cap lower on my head and glance out at Avery and Billie dancing.

I feel like an ass. Billie hasn't said a word to me since we left. In fact, she hasn't even looked at me once. It's like I don't exist.

I should be happy to be out; no one has recognised me yet, and having her keep her space is the ideal outcome, given that I can't have her, but instead of making me feel better it's just fuelling my rage.

Every shake of her hips or smile on her lips is just making me more pissed off. The worst part about it is I can't even have a drink, and I'm surrounded by it.

Josh tosses back another shot, catches my eye and grins, apparently oblivious to my mood.

He might be a pain in my ass, but I'd be lost without him. He's the only person in my inner circle that doesn't make allowances for my addiction. He drinks in front of me, and I need that, no matter how much it pisses me off. Alcohol doesn't just disappear because I can't drink it.

I guess the same could be said for Billie. Her and Avery are downing drinks like there's no tomorrow, but I'm not sure I'd count her as being in my inner circle, not yet – maybe not ever.

"You going to go and talk to her? Or would you rather stand here like a prick all night with a scowl on your face?"

"The latter," I growl, turning my head so I can't see the tempting brunette anymore.

"Well fuck that." He shrugs. "You can sulk all night, but I'm going to go make myself the filling in a hot-girl sandwich."

He yells out the girls' names and bounds towards them like a big golden retriever.

Billie finally glances at me, and I hold her gaze until she looks away, dropping her eyes to the floor.

"Fuck this," I mutter.

I'm agitated.

I'm on edge.

I know what I need. I don't know where I'm going to get it, but it sure as hell isn't standing here.

I give Oliver a gesture that I'll be back and skirt around the edge of the dancefloor before he can even think about following me.

He and Eric think they're blending in, but they stick out like dogs' balls in here. I'm probably more likely to get recognised with them hovering than I am without them.

I'm a hell of a lot more likely to pick up a chick without having a babysitter too.

I weave through the crowd, keeping my head down as I head for the less crowded area at the end of the bar.

I order a tonic water with lemon, because for some reason, women like to think that a guy is having a few drinks.

I lean against the bar for a few moments, taking in the scene around me.

There are women everywhere, but none that are anywhere near hot enough to fuck Billie out of my system.

I sip my bullshit drink and listen to some guy getting shot down a few spaces down from me.

I can't see the chick's face, but I don't miss the way her head shakes from side to side and how she's trying to subtly move away from him.

I smirk. *Watch and learn, buddy.*

I head for the girl, an arrogance in my swagger.

My smirk deepens when I finally lay eyes on her. Red-head, great rack and a skirt so short it makes Billie's look modest.

Her eyes drift from the dude she's trying to escape, to me, and the look of distaste turns into one of hunger.

She doesn't recognise me, I can see that, but she wants me all the same.

I jut my chin out conceitedly and a wicked grin crosses her lips as she slides from her seat and comes to meet me.

Maybe it won't be so hard to forget the woman I came here with after all.

I hold my hand out to her and she takes it without question, following me without hesitation to a dark, private corner of the club.

CHAPTER TWELVE

I feel the sweat running down between my boobs and I sigh heavily. I look around for Masen where I last saw him, but there's no sign of him anywhere.

Eric and Oliver haven't moved an inch, but Oliver, in particular, doesn't look happy. Eric is starting to make me feel self-conscious with how close he's watching me, but no doubt he's just following his orders.

"Where's Masen?" I yell at Josh over the thumping music.

He shrugs at me and continues grinding his crotch against my best friend's ass.

I don't know how that's considered dancing, but it seems like that's what they're going with.

"You good, B?" Avery shouts, worry marring her features as she takes in my concerned expression.

"I just... I hope he's not drinking or something," I yell back.

Josh scowls at the idea, and Avery looks surprised. "He wouldn't, would he?"

It's my turn to shrug now. I don't know anything much about Masen when it comes down to it. I'm in no way qualified to know how strong his resolve is.

"Fuck's sake, FG, now you've got me worried." Josh is doing what I just did, scanning the area where he left Masen, and coming up empty.

"You don't really think he'd..."

"Only one way to find out."

The music suddenly seems too loud, the pulsing dancefloor too crowded.

Josh shoves me in front of him and follows me through the crowd, towing Avery behind him.

"Where'd he go?" Josh demands when we reach Oliver and Eric.

"Disappeared into the crowd about a half hour ago." Oliver scowls.

I gape at him. He's got no idea where Masen is, and I have a bad feeling in the pit of my stomach.

"*Disappeared*? What the fuck is that shit? Isn't it your job to know where he is at all times?" Josh demands, his chest rising and falling heavily.

"It's my job to do whatever he tells me to do," Oliver replies, his tone less than impressed with Josh's accusations. "He told me to wait."

"Whatever, man."

Josh turns, reaching for my hand as he does, tugging me and Avery behind his big body. He pushes through the masses of people, his head turning side to side as he looks for his friend.

This is probably the first time he's had his hands on me that I actually approve of.

"Do you see him?" Avery asks, pushing up to her tip toes to try and see for herself.

It's not so loud over here – thank god – I can hear myself think for the first time in the past two hours, but there's no way

I'll be able to see if Avery can't, she's got about two inches on me.

"Nope. If that fucker has a drink, I'll kill him myself."

"He won't," I hear myself saying.

Josh spins around to look at me, dropping my hand as he goes. "What makes you so sure?"

I shrug a shoulder. "I mean... I hope he won't."

Josh mutters something under his breath and stares at me curiously as Avery scans the area looking for the man of the moment.

"Oh, you're *kidding* me," she hisses, her hands balling into fists at her sides.

My heart drops as I follow her line of sight to the darkest corner of this slimy nightclub, and there he is, reclined back against his seat, arms slung wide, an unlit cigarette dangling from his lips, and a beautiful redhead sitting in his lap.

She's giggling, throwing her head back with laughter, and touching his chest like she has the right to.

Avery steps in his direction but I grab her. "Don't, please, Avery," I beg, but she's not listening. She shakes off my hand and charges in the direction of Masen.

I don't want to go over there; the thought of seeing Masen up close with another woman makes my stomach roll, but Avery is about to cause a scene. Masen has gotten away with not being recognised this long, but that's all about to change if I don't rein her in.

"Oh shit," I hear Josh say, a hint of amusement in his tone. "He's about to cop it, isn't he?"

"You have no idea," I mutter as I rush after her.

I glance behind me and see that Eric and Oliver have both followed and, for the first time since this whole thing began, I'm glad they're here.

Oliver especially, because if I know my best friend – which I do – Masen is about to require protection.

I can feel Josh at my side as I skirt around the few people in my path, all the while watching Avery bulldoze her way to the man who is single-handedly destroying my heart and dignity.

Masen looks up from his piece of ass just in time to see Avery skid to a stop in front of him, and he looks right at her, his face expressionless.

"You're a real fucking asshole, you know that?" she screams at him. "What the hell is your problem?"

She doesn't know exactly what happened between the two of us earlier – him rejecting me – but she knows that *something* happened, that he did something to hurt me. She's also not blind, and you'd have to be to not have seen the chemistry sizzling between us this weekend.

She promised not to cause trouble, but I guess that promise went out the window the minute she saw him with someone else.

The red head in his lap glares at Avery and instinctively, I get my back up. I might be letting Masen treat me like shit, but no way is anyone crossing my best girl.

"Do you know this bitch?" she asks Masen, flipping her hair over her shoulder as she speaks.

Avery lunges forward, about to rip into the chick. I make a grab for her, but Josh is faster, tugging Avery's back against his front and wrapping his arms around her middle, holding her back.

"Chill, baby, they're not worth it… either of them." He spits the last part like venom.

I gasp at Josh's words and the look of disappointment on his face as he and Masen exchange unspoken words.

Avery half-heartedly struggles against him, sending a death glare Masen and the girl's way.

"You should get a leash for your cat," the red head says, grinning as she settles back into Masen's lap.

"That's really original." Avery sneers as Josh hauls her off, away from us, and then it's just me, standing there, hurting for something I never even had.

"You want something, sugar?" Masen asks, his tone lazy but his eyes burning with an emotion I've never seen on him.

Only to have never met you, I think to myself.

I take one final look at him, shake my head and walk away.

***

I don't let the tears fall until I make it to the bathroom. The last thing I need is for Masen or that stupid girl to see me cry.

I could do without Eric seeing me break down too. I don't need anyone else in this whole mess thinking that I'm weak.

A girl stumbles out of a stall behind me, and I swipe at the tear running down my cheek.

"Oh, babe, are you okay?" she asks in a typical 'I'm a drunk girl in a nightclub bathroom' way.

I nod, rather unconvincingly.

"Boy trouble," she states.

"How'd you know?" I sniff.

She rolls her eyes in an overly emphasised gesture. "Girls don't cry in the bathroom over anything else."

She's probably right about that too.

"You're a total babe. You should just go tell him to fuck himself and get yourself a new one."

I huff out a laugh. "It's slightly more complicated than that."

She turns the tap on and shoves her hands under the stream, sending water spraying all over her dress. She doesn't even seem to notice.

"He hot?"

"Scorching," I admit.

"Well then go get your man," she states and, honestly, I'm surprised she doesn't pair it with a few finger snaps.

She sways on her heels and, drunk as she is, she still might have a point.

As far as the world is concerned, he *is* my man.

That's *my* damn man out there, and no way am I going to be a doormat that sits around and lets myself be disrespected like that.

This whole thing might be pretend, but it was real enough that Josh wasn't allowed to kiss me. It's real enough that my privacy has been erased. I bet it would be real enough that no other guy would be allowed to come near me either, and if that's the case, it can be real now too.

I straighten my spine, and my resolve while I'm at it.

"You're right."

She waves her hand dismissively. "I'm always right after tequila shots."

I shoot her a grateful smile, check my makeup in the mirror and rush from the bathroom.

Josh, Avery and Eric are all waiting outside the door for me, but I walk straight past them.

"B!" Avery yells, but I don't even turn.

I'm on a mission now and I'm not stopping until Masen Lennox learns that I'm not going to be a woman he can walk all over.

I shove through the throngs of people until I reach the spot where I left Masen and his little side kick. Only now, he's alone.

"What? No lap accessory this time?" I demand, my tone sassy.

He looks up at me in surprise, his dark eyes finding mine in a flash.

"Why are you here?"

"I came to talk."

"About?"

"My conditions."

He rises from his seat slowly, his attention apparently piqued.

He slowly pulls the unlit cigarette from his lips and tucks it behind his ear, his ball cap now slung backwards on his head.

The action related to his dirty habit shouldn't turn me on, but *damn*, he makes being bad look so good.

He's too calm and composed as he steps towards me; it un-nerves me all over again.

I cross my arms across my chest and try to remember why I'm here – what I want from him.

"And what are your conditions, sugar?"

"If we're going to keep doing this... if you expect me to be 'your girl', then I have rules."

He smirks arrogantly, but waves for me to continue.

I look past him to the empty glass next to the chair he was occupying, there's no way of knowing what was in it just by looking at it. "No alcohol."

He follows my line of sight.

"Haven't touched a drop."

I meet his gaze again and I believe him. Undoubtedly, and maybe that makes me dumb, but I'm beginning to realise that even the smartest girls get a little dumb when faced with Masen Lennox.

"And no other women," I say while I still have the nerve.

The words hang between us.

"I have needs," he growls.

"So do I."

His stare grows heated. "What are you suggesting, sugar?"

I don't know what I'm suggesting, but the words fell from my lips before I could think them through and now that I've said them, implied what I have – I want it. I want it bad.

"You know what I'm suggesting." My voice wavers, but my eyes never leave his.

I want this. I want *him*.

He closes the distance between us, his lean body pressing against mine.

"You want to give me this sexy body?"

"Yes," I murmur, nerves going crazy in my chest.

"It's just sex – I can't give you more," he promises.

I nod slowly as he cups my jaw.

I can't think.

I don't care.

I only want.

"I'm your girl, use me," I whisper.

CHAPTER THIRTEEN

I'm your girl, use me.

The tempting words bounce around my mind as we drive back to the house.

Josh didn't even look at me. He's fucked off with me and I haven't seen him this pissed off in a while. Avery looked like she wanted to knee me in the balls, so I'm glad as hell they're not riding with us.

Josh and Avery are in one vehicle with Eric, and Billie is in the back of the Range Rover being driven by Oliver, with me.

I haven't spoken a word to her since she offered herself to me and I feel like a prick.

I don't like feeling like a prick. I don't like feeling anything at all. I like getting what I want from women and then cutting ties. No strings attached. No guilt. No feelings.

We both get what we need from the night and then we go our separate ways.

This is different.

That's not going to happen here, not with Billie.

There's the fact that she's a live-in deal, but it's even more complicated than that. She's not the kind of girl you fuck once and forget about. She's sexy in a way that she doesn't even know about yet. She's intriguing, and above all else, she's too fucking sweet.

I know myself, if I let anything or anyone get too close, especially someone like the woman sitting next to me, I'll get addicted.

It's who I am.

An addict.

And I have a feeling that the pull of alcohol would be nothing compared to the allure of Billie.

"Would you just say something?" She whispers the plea.

I exhale heavily.

I don't know what she wants me to say... how I can already imagine how it would feel to be inside her? How good I already know she tastes?

"If you're not attracted to me, you can just say so... I won't be offended. I know I'm not like that girl in the club."

I've got her seatbelt undone and her lifted into my lap before she even gets her sentence finished.

The fact that she's even considering her sex appeal to be the problem here is a situation I need to fix. *Right now.*

She gasps as I lift my hips, the hardness between my legs making itself known.

"*Masen*," she pleads and once again, my name on her lips is my complete undoing.

My hands thread into her long, silky hair, and I tug her mouth to mine in a rough, urgent kiss.

I kiss her like she's the only woman I've ever wanted this badly, and truthfully, if I'm honest with myself about her for one fucking second, she *is*.

I don't know what it is about my little sugar, but nothing has ever tasted so sweet.

Her hands grip my biceps, holding on tight as though she's afraid of falling.

Oliver speeds down the wide, open roads, either oblivious to the make-out session in his back seat, or just really fucking good at his job.

She pulls away, breathing hard before dropping her mouth to my jaw, placing kisses all the way up to my ear.

"If you think the problem is that *I* don't want *you*, then you're not as smart as I've given you credit for."

The problem is that I want her too much – and it's a real fucking issue.

She leans back, searching my eyes for a hint of bullshit. Finding none, she nods.

I don't know what it is about this girl, but no one has been able to read me the way she can – not even Josh, and he sees way too much.

"Are you going to turn me away again?" she asks, her voice raspy. She's trying, but she can't hide the hurt completely.

I fucking hate that I hurt her. I hate that I care too. I don't want to care.

I could explain to her why I turned her down earlier, when I so easily could have taken her, but that's only going to complicate this mess further.

I don't know what the fuck to do.

I do know one thing though, there's no way I'm turning her down again.

I might be an asshole, but I'm not an idiot.

"Fuck no, sugar," I growl. "You're mine."

"That's what the world believes."

"You wait until I get you in my bed. You'll believe it too."

Her breath catches and I take the opportunity to capture her soft, sweet lips again.

She's too good for me, I can feel it in her kiss, but I'm known for being a selfish bastard, so it won't stop me from taking her anyway. I've got a reputation to uphold.

"We're here," I murmur as the car slows and stops.

She nods and lifts one of her sexy legs to climb off my lap.

I trap her, my hands landing on her thighs, and she gasps again.

I grin, a real, full fucking grin. I can't help it. If just my hands on her bare skin get her this on edge, I can't even imagine the fun I'm about to have with her.

"Did you just smile?" she breathes.

"Maybe."

"I've never seen you smile, not like that."

"Don't get used to it," I growl as the door next to me opens and I shuffle, her still in my lap, and swing us around so I can climb out.

She tries to scramble down, but fuck that, if I'm finally going to give in and have her, I'm not going to half-ass it.

"Stop squirming, sugar," I mutter as I bury my face in the crook of her neck and bite down gently.

She moans and her arms and legs clamp around me tightly, allowing me to carry her inside.

She drops her face to my shoulder. "This is *so* embarrassing."

I have the urge to laugh, but I suppress it. She's just seen me smile; I'll be screwed if she gets a laugh out of me too.

"Oliver can see us," she hisses, her mortification obvious.

Fuck it all, I grin again.

This girl...

Too fucking sweet.

***

I carry her into my room, ignoring the stares from both Josh and Avery as we pass them in the living room.

I don't even think Billie sees; her face is still buried into my neck.

I kick my door shut behind us and glance around the messy room.

It might not be my usual bed, the one at my house, but it's a bed of mine, in a house of mine, so that's going to have to be close enough to my fantasies for tonight.

I let go of her thighs and she slides down my body, coaxing a moan from my throat.

She feels so good, I don't know how the fuck I'm ever going to be able to stop.

Her feet land on the floor, and she looks up at me with wide, trusting, hazel eyes.

I don't deserve that look. I've done nothing but be cold to her, hurt her, keep her at arm's length.

I probably would have screwed that chick at the club tonight if she hadn't have come back and thrown around her demands like a sexy little tiger. All bark and no bite.

I'm an asshole, plain and simple, but as long as she knows that – accepts that about me – then I can handle what I am.

Even though we both know she's got a legally binding con-tract that states she doesn't have a leg to stand on, I'll agree to her terms, because I need her – not just to save my career... but

I need to do this with her. I need her here with me, not someone else – *her*.

So as long as she's here there won't be anyone else.

No one but her.

She licks her lips, and I know I should say something, *anything* to reassure her about what comes next, but I'm coming up blank.

She shakes her head, almost as though she knows what's going through my mind and she's telling me that words aren't needed.

Good.

I've never been much of a talker anyway, I've always been about the lyrics, the beat, the melody. I could never talk another day in my life as long as I could sing.

She pushes up to her tip toes, all pure and innocent and presses her lips to mine.

I hope like hell I'm not about to take her virginity, but I'm not asking. No fucking way. Not with the way her hands are roaming under my shirt and down to my waistband, because if she says this is her first time, I still won't stop, and then I *really* will be the biggest bastard in the world.

I find the zip at her back and lower it, she wiggles free of the straps and the sexy little outfit falls to the floor at her feet, just like it was before we went out tonight, back when I *should* have claimed her.

I hold her out at arm's length so I can look at her, really fucking look at her, because a body like that deserves to be appreciated.

She's been driving me crazy all weekend. Her tiny bikinis leave nothing to the imagination, yet somehow, she looks even better than I thought possible.

The only sound in the room is my laboured breathing as I take her in.

She turns in a slow circle, allowing me my fill.

Fuck.

I'm so screwed.

If alcohol is my addiction, this girl is my kryptonite.

She reaches for the buttons on my shirt warily, like she's worried it's all going to disappear again, but fuck that. I'm in. I'm *all in*. Consequences, reputation and career be damned. Right now, they all pale in comparison to the want I have for her.

I couldn't stop if I tried.

I rip at my shirt, tugging it from my body. The buttons fly across the room as they pop from the fabric, and she smirks.

I tug roughly on my belt and it's sliding out from the loops of my jeans in a flash, falling to the floor to keep her scrap of clothing company.

Her hands meet mine and she undoes the button on my jeans, followed by the zip with a swiftness that makes me think I might have underestimated her innocence.

I lift my hands behind my head and stand there, appreciating the view as she tugs my jeans down my thighs, wasting no time in taking my boxer briefs with them too.

A throaty rumble comes out my mouth as she crouches, licking her lips at the sight of my hard dick, standing at attention just for her.

Jesus, I want those plump lips wrapped around my cock like you wouldn't believe, but not tonight, I haven't got the self-control for that right now.

I reach for her hand and she takes it without hesitation. I tug her back to her feet, and she falls heavily against me, my hard length resting against her stomach.

She swallows deeply, her nerves warring with her. I reach behind her and unsnap her bra, ridding her of it before she gets a chance to overthink this.

She's looking at me again with those trusting eyes, and for a second I let myself believe that I could be worthy of that trust.

I pretend to be something I'm not as I drag her underwear down her legs, peppering her legs with kisses as I trail down her body.

I act like the man she deserves as I lower her onto the bed, and as I push into her, right to the hilt, she calls out my name like that's exactly the man I am.

CHAPTER FOURTEEN

Billie

I pause in the doorway and listen carefully.

He's singing again.

I rest my head against the hallway wall and stay as still as I can.

If he hears me, he'll stop. That's what happened yesterday, and the day before.

Every morning since we got back from the beach house, he's been working on a new song.

He hums a section that he hasn't filled with lyrics, and I smile as I hear him drumming his fingers on the kitchen benchtop, trying to figure out a melody that works.

He's so close to putting it all together, I can feel it. I wish he'd let me hear everything he has all together, rather than the bits and pieces I've managed to sneak when he doesn't know I'm here, but apparently he meant it when he said it was just sex between us and nothing more.

Just sex seems like such an insufficient phrase for what happened between us the past few days, I knew he'd be good in bed, I *did*, but I could never have prepared myself for the chemistry between us.

He's touched, kissed and worshipped every inch of my body, but he still hasn't let me into his head.

Sometimes it feels like he wants to, but he holds back, giving me only glimpses of what we could share.

I sigh as he floats through a verse and hits what I'm sure will become the chorus in time.

I don't know about him, but I can hear it... the melody, the flow... I can imagine how it could sound, and it would be *incredible*.

In fact, I can hear it so clearly that I *have* to do something about it.

I slip past the doorway, leaving him softly crooning and rush down to the studio. I haven't been back down here since that first time with Josh. I know Masen likes his privacy, but I figure if I'm allowed in his bed then I'm allowed down here too.

I adjust a few dials, press the right buttons, enter the booth and reach for the acoustic guitar on the wall, bringing it into my lap as I slide onto the small stool.

I hit record and strum the first chord, then the next and the next.

My eyes drift closed, and I smile as I hear it coming together exactly the way I imagined it when I heard him sing it.

I tap the loop machine, set the guitar down and move for the keyboard, overlaying another element to the tune that's only becoming more fluid.

I'm no singer, but I can't help myself, I fill in the parts I have memorised from eavesdropping on Masen as the melody takes over.

My voice trails off at the section he was having trouble with and I frown, my eyes closed again. It sounds like a love song, but the bit where he really needs to commit – go all in – that's where he's struggling. My fingers continue to float over the keys, trying and failing to come up with anything that might fix it.

"What the hell was that, sugar?" his gruff voice startles me.

My fingers hit the keys out of time at the same moment my eyes fly open.

He's standing at the bottom of the stairs, his shoulder resting casually against the wall and his arms crossed loosely across his chest, but there's nothing casual about the fire burning in his eyes.

I can't decide if I'm in trouble or not.

"I... I, uh..." I jump up and hit the button to stop the loop recording. "Sorry, I just, I heard you..."

He raises a brow but says nothing as I stutter.

"I heard you in the kitchen and I felt the melody, you know? I just couldn't leave it. I'm sorry, I shouldn't have touched your stuff."

He pushes off the wall, and I stand, exiting the booth as quickly as I came in.

He strolls toward me, cutting off my exit. "You didn't tell me you played." It's an accusation.

I shove a loose strand of hair behind my ear. "I don't," I whisper as he comes close enough to touch me.

He stands tall, looming over me. "Sure as fuck sounded like you do."

I shrug and finally look up at him, meeting his dark eyes. He looks intrigued.

He reaches out slowly and touches my arm, his fingers trailing down from my elbow to my wrist, leaving a trail of fire in their wake.

"Tell me, sugar," he coaxes, his voice husky, and I'm a goner. I can't deny him what he wants when he talks to me like that.

"I've played guitar and piano since I was a kid, I'm not very good, but I play," I tell him quietly.

He nods thoughtfully. "You played my song."

I try to swallow the lump in my throat. I'm so nervous, my stomach is doing summersaults.

"It's a good song."

He opens his mouth to say something but thinks twice about it.

I catch the hand still trailing up and down my arm and entwine his fingers with mine.

He looks at our joined hands curiously, and it makes me wonder if anyone has ever held his hand before.

"Masen, I –"

"You need to go dress shopping," he interrupts me.

"I do?"

"You do."

"Okay," I reply, confused by his sudden change of topic.

He steps back and drops my hand.

"Why do I need a dress?"

"We're going to a movie premiere tomorrow night."

I can feel my eyes lighting up. "We are?"

He almost smiles, *almost*. "I worked on the soundtrack."

"And you're taking *me*?" I ask, my excitement growing.

This time he does smile, and it's the most beautiful thing I've ever seen. I wish he'd do it more often.

He reaches out and tucks the strand of hair that's found its way loose again, behind my ear. "You're my girl."

The way he says those three words makes my insides quiver. It's too easy to forget this is all make believe.

I nod stupidly, at a loss for words as he moves to let me past. I walk on shaky legs towards the stairs.

"Oh and, sugar?"

"Yeah?"

"Buy some longer shorts while you're there."

I turn and frown at him. "What? Why? I thought you liked my shorts."

He shakes his head, his expression pained. "Because as good as you look in those tiny little things, the idea of another man imagining you *out* of them makes me want to put my fist through a wall."

"Oh." The word falls from my lips, nothing following it through my shock.

"Yeah. *Oh.*"

I nod, once, twice, three times as I contemplate his words.

If I didn't know better, I'd think Masen Lennox just sounded jealous.

***

"He's going to go crazy when he sees you in that dress." Avery swoons, clutching the box containing a ridiculously expensive pair of shoes in it to her chest.

"I can carry that for you, Ma'am, it's really no problem," Eric tells her but she shushes him.

"I'm probably never going to get this close to a pair of Louboutin's ever again, Eric, let me have my moment, dammit."

He chuckles and shakes his head in amusement.

I've never spent so much money in one afternoon, and if it weren't for Avery being here, I probably would have ditched these high-end stores by now and gone to find something that costs a fraction of the price, but she wasn't having it.

Apparently if I'm going to be on the arm of a super star, I need to be dressed in thousands of dollars' worth of clothing and jewellery.

I'm almost scared to wear the diamond earrings that are on loan to me for the event. I've never held something so valuable.

We exit the store and Eric hands off the dress bags and various other shopping bags to a member of the security team. I have no idea how many of them are here with us, and I'm not sure I want to. Even Eric thinks it's overkill – I can tell by the tick of his jaw every time someone talks to him through his earpiece.

I'm a nobody, I don't need a team of big, burly men to protect me, but from what I can gather, there was no telling Masen that.

"Ma'am," Eric prompts, indicating to Avery's full hands.

She reluctantly hands over the shoes, her bottom lip sticking out in a pout. "You have to let me borrow those," she says, looping her arm through mine and towing me off towards another store.

"They're not mine, they're Masen's, you'll have to ask him."

She huffs out a laugh. "Oh yeah, I'm sure they'll look really good on him."

I roll my eyes. "He paid for them."

"Pffft, so what? He's got plenty of money. They're yours. When you guys go your separate ways, it'll be like a divorce where one person gets the dog, except it'll be a really expensive pair of pretty shoes." She sighs dreamily, and I feel my heart rate accelerate.

I don't want to think about going my separate way from Masen. I don't know what the hell is going on with me, but I'm starting to wish that his reputation would stay shitty so I'd have reason to stay longer, and that's a stupid, dangerous mindset to find myself in.

"But what am I saying? When you are a free woman, you'll have a million bucks to play with, so you can just buy me a pair of my own."

It takes me a minute to figure out what she's talking about and that's when I remember that not only is this fake, but I'm being *paid* to do it.

My stomach twists at the thought but I do my best to settle it. I can't think about this as anything other than a business deal with a side of red-hot sex.

Sleeping with Masen is a perk, nothing more.

I need to remember that.

"You know, you keep hooking up with Josh and you might find yourself rich and married before you know it."

She squeezes my arm and shrieks. "Honestly, B, that boy..." she fans her face, "he is *hung*, I've never seen a pe–"

"Please stop," I beg.

She giggles. "Sorry, but he is just... *wow*."

"So you like him then?" I press, eager to talk about something that isn't me and Masen.

"Not as much as you like the rock star."

I feel myself blush; so much for not talking about me. She's probably right, but I deny it anyway.

She rolls her eyes but allows the lie to slide.

"Yeah, I like him. He's sexy and fun, but he's a player, plain and simple. We're just having fun..." She half shrugs and it's obvious to see that she wishes there were a little more to it than that.

Don't we all.

She points to the Gucci sign, but I shake my head rapidly. I'm done with designer labels. I'm going to give a shop attendant a heart attack if I walk into another one of those fancy stores with my beat-up chucks on. I tug her past quickly before she can make it to the door.

"Hold up, did you just say that Josh is loaded?" she demands.

I smirk. I was waiting for that.

"Not that it matters," she backtracks quickly, "but I was under the impression he just mooches off Masen twenty-four seven."

"That's what he wants people to think." I pull her in the direction of my favourite discount chain store. "He's a game designer. He's killing it with some X-box game or whatever, I dunno... he wouldn't tell me much, but Morris said he's got his own mansion about fifteen minutes away from Masen's."

She gapes at me. "You're shitting me?"

"I shit you not."

"That little asshole! We went out for milkshakes last night and he said he forgot his wallet, made me pay. He slept over at my house, said his house was small!"

I giggle. That sounds like the Josh I'm coming to know well.

"Wait, why are we going into this cheap-ass store?" She screws up her face in distaste.

Classic Avery; one afternoon like a rich bitch with Masen's credit card and she's turned into a complete snob.

"I need some longer shorts."

She lets go of my arm and appraises me from head to toe. "What's wrong with the shorts you've got?"

"Masen kinda went all alpha male on me, told me he didn't want other guys seeing me in such tiny ones." I feel my cheeks heating again.

She gives me a look that says, 'I told you so'.

"He doesn't like me, not like that!" I insist, already knowing where this is heading. "It's all about appearances."

"Mmm hmmm, sure," she says. "C'mon girl, we're getting new shorts alright, but I can tell you one thing, they're only about to get shorter."

I groan as I trail in after her, Eric right behind me.

I should have known better than to tell Avery anything.

CHAPTER FIFTEEN

Masen

I hit play on the sound board and sit back, listening as the music she created floats through the air around me.

It's good, it's really fucking good.

She's got an ear for it, that's for sure.

I've been struggling over this song, the melody, for days. That might not seem like a lot, but usually when inspiration hits, it's down, done and dusted within twenty-four hours and I'm handing over a sample to Chuck the next day.

But this song, this one isn't playing ball. *Wasn't*, until I heard what she did – watched her doing it.

I close my eyes and rake my hands over my face.

It's all there now, playing out in my head like the next hit single.

I don't know how I feel about it. On the one hand, this is the first thing I've written since I got out of rehab, and I'm fucking glad I've still got it, but on the other hand, inspiration for it hit at two in the morning when Billie was curled into my side, wearing nothing but one of my shirts, and that can't mean anything good.

I've tried for days to talk myself out of the lyrics, the vibe, but it isn't working. The words were there whether I liked it or not, and it's a ballad... a fucking love song.

I don't write love songs, I'm not loved, and I don't love. It's as simple as that.

This song, though, *fuck*... it's got me all kinds of screwed up.

I don't love Billie, I'm not sure I'm capable of such a thing, but my creative brain didn't get that message.

I toss the pencil I've been furiously scribbling down lyrics and chords with and run my hand through my hair in frustration.

I don't know what the fuck is wrong with me.

She left for school first thing this morning, and I've checked the time every half an hour since.

It's fucking quiet here without her. I miss her noise...

It's not like when Josh is over, where you just wish he'd fuck off back to his place and give you some peace and quiet. When Billie is here, I can feel it – and I like knowing someone is here.

I know she's shopping with Avery now, Eric is keeping me regularly informed, but my fingers keep hovering over the reply button, tempting me to text him and tell him I need her back here for something.

I close my eyes and let my head fall back against the couch.

I picture her instantly. I can't help it; she's there every time my lids shut, and not even just images of me fucking her either, she's there in my kitchen, nervously watching and waiting for me to speak, or smiling at me when she doesn't think I'm paying attention.

I can picture her lying in the sun next to my pool, I can hear her singing in the shower when she thinks the spray of the water drowns the sound out.

Fuck.

I need to get my head on straight before I do something stupid like catch feelings for the girl.

My girl. My brain corrects me.

My phone rings and I grab it, seeing Chuck's name on the screen.

"Yeah?" I say as I grab the pencil again and start doodling on the sides of the paper.

"Just checking in."

I wait a few beats for him to speak up, tell me whatever the fuck it is he called to say.

"How's it going with the girl?"

I click my tongue. "Billie. Her name is Billie. And good."

"Good? That's high praise from you."

"It's fine, whatever, it's not like it's hard to sit around here and do shit all."

He's silent for a moment.

"You think she's ready for tomorrow night?"

Do I think that Billie can act like the doting girlfriend in front of the press? Yeah, yeah I do. The fact that it barely feels like she's acting is what really concerns me.

"She's got it."

"You fucked her yet?"

"No, what the fuck?" I demand too quickly, his question catching me off guard.

He groans. "You have. Fucking hell, Masen, I gave you one instruction."

It's my turn to be silent now.

"This isn't going to end well, I'm telling you, man."

"She knows the deal. She's cool with it."

"The fact that you believe that is what shits me the most."

"Leave it," I tell him, my tone final.

"Fine." He blows out a breath. "But when it all goes tits up, don't ask me to fix it for you."

I hang up the phone and toss it onto the seat next to me.

It's not until I glance at the sheet of paper in front of me that I realise I've named my latest song.

"Fuck," I mutter as I look at the word 'Sugar' staring back at me.

Chuck is right. This isn't going to end well.

***

She shrieks as I step out from the shadows and lift her ass onto the table.

"Masen, you scared me."

I settle between her legs, watching her heaving chest rise and fall.

"I got Avery's message," I rasp.

She blushes scarlet and tugs her bottom lip into her mouth, nibbling it while she thinks through her response.

"I told her not to send that," she finally says, her chin dropping to avoid my eyes. She's embarrassed by the sexy photo of her wearing sweet fuck all, but she shouldn't be – half the women in the world would probably kill to look that good doing it.

I push closer to her and her arms come up to rest around my neck.

"It was sexy as hell, sugar."

She glances back up, her hazel eyes focused on me again. "It was?"

I growl deep in my throat. "I've been going crazy waiting for you to get home ever since she sent it."

I hate the way it sounds, *home* and *her* in the same sentence, like it's right.

She smiles sweetly. "You been waiting on me, Masen Lennox?"

There's just the right mix of sass and innocence in her tone.

"I have," I answer honestly, for once in my god damn life.

"I like that."

I sure as shit don't, but it is what it is.

"What are you going to do with me now that you've got me?" Her fingers tease the hair at the back of my head, and I resist the urge to purr like a fucking kitten.

I chuckle darkly. "You can't even imagine."

She slides forward and I feel her feet cross behind me, at my ass.

She wants me to carry her, and I'm only too happy to oblige.

We walk, her in my arms, our eyes locked until I reach the couch, and I drop down, sitting with her nestled in my lap.

She tips her head, her long dark hair spilling over her shoulder, covering one of her eyes.

What a fucking sight she is.

"I finished the song," I say before I can even think it through.

She stills, her eyes widening. "You did?" she asks hesitantly.

I know why she's treading carefully – this is the first scrap of information about my music that I've ever offered her willingly.

I nod.

"I bet it's amazing," she whispers, and the fact that she doesn't push me for more, only makes me want to give it to her.

Silence envelopes us. It's dark out; the moonlight is reflected on the surface of the pool. Morris has been given the night off, with the intention that Billie and I might want some privacy in not particularly private areas of this house.

She follows my line of sight out the big, open glass doors and sighs, content.

"I worked it out with your melody."

Her eyes flash back to mine. "Are you serious?"

"Do I ever joke?"

She shakes her head, and fuck it pleases me greatly that she felt like she could answer that question this time.

"No. I think you could though."

I tilt my head, studying her face curiously.

"Joke I mean..." she insists. "I don't think you want to be so serious all the time. I see that curve in your lips when you don't think I'm looking. I hear your laughter when you think you're out of earshot. You don't fool me, Mase."

I both hate and love how well she seems to know me after only such a short time. It feels suspiciously like letting someone get close to me, and that's not something I'm willing to allow.

"Mase?" I question, picking up on her casual use of the nickname.

She pops a shoulder. "I figure if you get to call me *sugar* all the time, the least I can do is drop a letter from your name."

I drop my head back, eyes closed. Shit. *Nicknames*. Next we'll have a fucking couple name – if the public haven't given us one already, and people will be *shipping* us or whatever the fuck it is they do these days.

I should call time on this. Chuck is one hundred percent right – it's not going to end well.

She weaves her fingers into my hair and tugs my head forward. "Don't run," she pleads, her eyes begging. "Not from me."

I want to. I've got the urge to close off and run further and faster than ever before, but there's one thing keeping me from doing it and that's the woman in my arms...

I can't leave her. I can't shut her out. Physically and mentally, I can't force myself to do it. Not yet anyway.

"*Masen*," she whispers.

No way can I run out on her now, not with my name falling from her lips.

So I do the next best thing, one of the things I'm finest at, and I capture her lips with mine.

CHAPTER SIXTEEN

Billie

I pad out of the bathroom and slide back into the bed before he can do something stupid like suggest that I go back to my own room.

I can't. I *won't*.

Not after what just happened between us, first on the couch downstairs, and then again in his bed.

We *connected*.

That didn't feel like 'just sex', that felt like making love. A stupid thought. Boys like Masen Lennox don't make love, they *fuck*, but I don't know how else to explain the adoring look in his eyes, or the way he handled me with total tenderness.

I snuggle into his side, wrapping my arm around his toned middle.

He freezes, and just when I think I'm about to get kicked out, he lifts his arm, allowing me closer before draping it around me.

"Are you scared?" I ask as he twists a strand of my hair around his finger.

"About what?" he asks, his voice husky – the way I love it.

"The premiere tomorrow... seeing everyone after what happened last time?"

Technically it's tonight, but that's not the point.

I feel him shake his head and I twist, my head on his shoulder so I can see his face.

"They're just people, sugar – they've all got their dirty little secrets. Most of them are just better at hiding them than I am."

"I'm really proud of how you took responsibility for your problems, Masen. It takes a big man to admit when he fucked up."

It's his turn to turn now, so we're laying side by side, facing one another.

This is the most open, exposed and vulnerable I've ever seen him – it's like he's dropped the wall and I'm almost too scared to breathe in case he realises and slaps it back up.

"You're proud of me?"

I nod, my hand snaking up to trace the line of his jaw. "Are you not proud of yourself?"

He grunts, it's not a yes or a no.

"I bet there are a lot of people who are proud of you."

He huffs out a disbelieving laugh.

"Oh c'mon," I soothe, "what about your family?"

I watch his jaw tick as he slowly swallows. "I don't have family."

I hear my sharp intake of breath. "*What*?"

"I'm a foster kid, sugar. My mumma was a drug addict and she didn't even know who my dad was. I bounced around from placement to placement, nowhere ever really stuck."

That breaks my heart. Damn near tears me in two.

I can't imagine not having the support of my parents. They might live on the other side of the country, but they'd do anything for me, including not asking questions when I told them I was dating a recently recovering alcoholic superstar.

His dark eyes stare at me, hard, willing me to give him the sympathy I'm sure he's come to expect.

"You have family, Masen. Maybe not by blood, but you have family."

He's blows out a breath – the same way he does when I've watched him smoke a cigarette.

"Well where the fuck have they been then? Because I haven't seen anyone."

"I see them... I see Chuck making arrangements that go beyond the scope of his job... I see Josh here every second day, sleeping on your couch or in your pool house when he has a perfectly good house of his own to go to."

He huffs out another laugh, but the hardness in eyes wavers.

"You don't really think he comes over here so often because he has nothing better to do, do you? He's here for *you*, Masen, because he's worried about you – because you're his family... he loves you."

I think I might too. I think it, but I'm in no way brave enough to voice it aloud.

He doesn't say a word, just looks into my eyes, his mind ticking over.

There's a softness inside of him that he doesn't let out often, if ever. It's covered in suspicion and buried in arrogance, but I see it, just a little peek at a time.

He wants the world – me included – to see him a certain way, but that's not the real him. The real him is tender, warm, kind and protective. The real him is the man in front of me, reluctant as he is to make an appearance.

The real him is the man who won't let me set a foot outside this house without a huge, hulking bodyguard. The real him cares.

"We should get some sleep," he says, his voice gravelly and thick.

I nod, lean forward and press a soft kiss to the corner of his mouth. "Goodnight, Mase."

I think I see him flash a grin, but it's gone just as quickly.

"Goodnight, sugar."

***

"Sugar," Masen barks, and both Ange and I jump.

I look to her, but she's got her head back in her work before we even make eye contact.

"What?" I breathe.

"Stop the knee jiggling," he demands. "It's making me nervous.

My eyes flash to my knee and sure enough, it's bouncing like crazy.

I rest my hand on it and it stops.

"Sorry, I'm kind of freaking out."

"*Kind of freaking out.*" He all but rolls his eyes. "Sugar, you're way past that."

"Sorry," I squeak as I glance out the window.

I don't know how he's so calm. This movie premiere isn't just any movie – it's starring some of the biggest names in the world.

People so famous I want to puke. People like him.

He might be used to rubbing shoulders with the planet's rich and famous, but I'm not. I'm a nobody.

"I shouldn't be here, I don't belong," I say on an exhale, my voice barely audible.

He leans forward in his seat where he sits, facing me, Ange at his side.

He looks so fucking handsome in his tux. I never would have expected it, given how good I think he looks in ripped jeans and a faded tee, but hell, he wears the shit out of that thing.

Ange nudges his side. "I think I should run her through it."

"No," he snaps. "She's got this."

I'm really not sure I do, but his confidence in me is reassuring.

"Look at me," he demands, and my eyes fly from his chest to his face. "You think *I* belong here?"

I nod.

He shakes his head.

"You do," I argue. "You're talented, you have something to offer these people. I'm just some girl someone picked out in an office."

I know Ange is watching us, the furious scribbling of her pen is absent, but I can't pull my eyes from his to check.

He reaches out and my hands meet his without even thinking about it.

"It wasn't just *someone* who picked you, sugar."

I swallow deeply, hung up on his every word.

"It was me. *I* picked you. I picked you because I wanted you here. Because you should be here. Because you belong."

This is the most he's ever said to me. It's the closest he's ever come to letting me believe he might feel something for me even remotely close to what I'm starting to feel for him.

"Okay," I whisper.

"I won't leave your side. The whole night."

"You promise?" I ask quietly as the car pulls up to a stop.

"Fucking promise."

He grips my hands tighter and then his door is opened, and the flashing lights start going wild.

He slides out of the car, his hand reaching back for me the only part of him I can see.

Ange is looking at me with a mixture of curiosity and shock.

"What?" I whisper as I check I'm covered in all the right places; the last thing I need is a boob slip when half the world is probably watching.

She shakes her head. "It's just... he's different with you."

That's all I get out of her before Masen's head appears back in the car, impatient as ever.

"You comin' out of there?"

I nod, eager to be closer to him, and he winks at me, fucking winks, his dark glossy hair falling in his eyes.

I suck in a breath as he gently coaxes me from the car.

I stand, a little wobbly on my feet as the enormity of what I've just stepped into becomes obvious.

There are people *everywhere*, and they're all screaming Masen's name.

It's *crazy*.

I can feel Ange mucking around with the back of my dress and I go to glance over my shoulder, but Masen catches my jaw between his fingers, halting me.

"She's got it," he whispers, for only me to hear.

He holds my face so close to his and that familiar warmth settles in my belly, setting me on fire in only a way he seems to know how.

He leans in and I gasp. I never expected him to kiss me in front of all these people, but he does, god he does, and when his lips leave mine, I'm breathless.

"I'm really glad you're here with me, sugar," he murmurs.

I smile against his lips.

It's probably the nicest thing he's ever said to me, and it had nothing to do with my ass or my shorts, so it's probably the most genuine too.

I swear he smiles back, but he's too close for me to really tell, and before I know it, I'm being led, Masen's hand in mine, down the red carpet to the photographers, who are all yelling, trying to get Masen to look their way. He stops for no more than ten seconds each before moving on – this isn't his first rodeo, that much is clear.

Each time he pauses, I'm tucked against his side and his eyes find mine, not the lens they're all begging him to look at.

He's looking at me in a way that makes goosebumps break out on my skin as we stop again, posing for yet another picture. I don't even know what I'm doing, I just know I can't take my eyes off his long enough to even smile.

"Did I tell you how fucking perfect you look in that dress?" he asks and my heart thumps erratically against my rib cage.

I give my head a small shake.

The 'fucking hell, sugar' that he choked out when I came downstairs and he saw me for the first time gave me a pretty good indication that he liked what he saw, but those words he's just said now, they're even more welcome to my ears.

"Well you do," he whispers, tugging me closer, and I don't know how, given that we're surrounded by people, but he makes me feel like it's just the two of us.

"Two compliments in one evening, better watch out, someone will get wind that you're a big softy on the inside."

He grins, but it's not sweet, it's menacing, and hell if that doesn't get me more hot and bothered than his tender side.

"You think I'm soft, sugar?" he teases, his big warm hand pressing into the small of my back, pulling me even closer to him.

I nod slowly, caught up in what he might do next.

"Better show everyone how bad I really am then," he growls as he captures my mouth in a kiss so hot I melt against him, my perfectly manicured nails digging into his shoulders.

I hear shutters clicking and people screaming in excitement, but all I can really focus on is him, the music world's bad boy.

He breaks the kiss, his chest heaving as he dips his head to rest his forehead against mine.

"Well, fuck," I mutter.

He pulls back, holding me so he can search my face – oblivious to every person calling his name – did you just say *fuck*, sugar?"

"I did."

A slow grin spreads across his face and, *wow*, it's the most spectacular thing I've ever seen, I'm rendered speechless by it, in fact.

He chuckles and tucks me back against his side, his arm coming around me.

Holy shit. Masen Lennox just smiled. At *me*.

I swallow deeply.

One single smile and I know for sure... I'm completely in love with him.

CHAPTER SEVENTEEN

Masen

I glance at her over the top of the book I've been pretending to read for the past half an hour.

I need time to think, to process, and I need to be away from her to do it, but every time I contemplate walking away, my feet don't move.

I'm stuck. Stuck here looking at her in that tiny pink bikini.

I can't even escape to my room because it still smells like her. Her dress is thrown over the chair in the corner and her underwear is left torn on the floor.

That's not exactly the space I need... *fuck*, I'm hard again just thinking about it.

"Why don't you ever take your shirt off out here?" she asks absently, and I lower the book further.

She's got dark shades on, and I can't tell if her eyes are open or closed.

"What?"

"I've been here what? Two months? And not once have I seen you with your shirt off."

I cock a brow at her, and she blushes a deep red.

"You know what I mean."

I shrug. "I'm not Josh, I don't feel the need to parade my shit all over."

She sits up, tucking her long, lean legs beneath her. "Masen Lennox, are you self-conscious because of Joshy's rock-hard six-pack?"

I scowl at her. "Fuck no."

"You *are*." She giggles like it's the funniest joke she's ever heard, and I have to fight to keep the corners of my mouth from turning up.

"I am fucking not," I bite back, sliding to the edge of my lounger and throwing my legs off the side so I'm facing her.

"What's the problem then, big shot?"

I smirk. "You ever seen any tan lines on me, sugar?"

She thinks about it for a moment before shaking her head slowly, *cautiously,* as though she might be walking into some kind of trap.

I lean in closer and she mimics me automatically.

"Think about that for a minute."

She narrows her eyes at me and frowns. "The only way to get no tan lines would be to walk around nude." She huffs out a laugh before realisation dawns as a devious smirk grows on her face. "Oh well, by all means, don't let me keep you from what you're used to."

She pulls the shades from her face and tosses them onto the towel next to her like she's ready for a show.

I shake my head and push forward so I'm hovering over her.

She gasps and falls back, I move closer again, not willing to give her an inch.

"What do you think would happen if I started taking my clothes off, huh?" I rake my eyes over her barely-covered body, and she shudders. "You think we'd still be sitting here relaxing?"

She reaches up, her palm sliding across my t-shirt-covered chest and around the back of my neck. "I hope not," she breathes.

She tugs, hard, and I fall onto her, our mouths meeting in a flash.

Shit, she feels too good, smells too nice, tastes too fucking sweet...

"Get a room, dude." Josh's voice comes from behind me, and I groan.

Billie's ankles are crossed behind my back and when I stand, she comes with me, gripping my neck like a vice as I sit us down on my lounger.

Josh watches us, a wide, easy smile on his lips.

He likes me and Billie together, I can tell. I don't know what the hell I'm going to do about that when this is all over, but I'll worry about that later.

I've got no space in my head for anything else right now.

His eyes flick from mine to Billie's. "You better get in there. She made me buy her every gossip magazine known to man and she's tipping them fucking everywhere."

Billie frowns, and I study her closely, totally engrossed in the way her features move when she speaks. "What? Who?"

"Your BFF. Thanks for spilling your guts about me being rich by the way, that was a real dick move."

I watch as she rolls her eyes. "*No*, making a poor student pay for all your food was a dick move, but that's not the point, *why* is she collecting that trash?"

Josh chuckles, and a part of me hates the way they interact so effortlessly, so fucking easily, like they've been friends for years.

"You're on the cover of damn near every magazine, FG."

Her back straightens. "Shut up, I am *not*."

"You *are*." He chuckles as she scrambles from my lap. "Looking like a stone-cold fox, I might add."

"Thank you, Joshy." She smiles as she passes by him, her sexy ass swaying all the way into my house. He high-fives her, and I have to stop myself from giving him a warning about touching what's mine again.

I lay back on my seat, throwing on my sunglasses once she's out of sight, and wait for him to come and hassle me – he's bound to, it's what he does best.

"Never thought I'd see the day." He chuckles as he takes his position on my left.

And here we go...

"What's that?" I drawl lazily.

"The day you finally caught feelings for a chick. I gotta say, man, I didn't think it was gonna happen, but she's good for you – shit she might even be the best thing."

"It hasn't happened. There's no feelings."

"You expect me to believe that?"

"It's the truth."

He huffs out a laugh. "You clearly haven't seen the pictures from last night."

"What does that have to do with anything?"

I watch out the corner of my eye as he pulls out his cell phone, taps away for a few seconds and then holds it out for me to look at.

I snag it from his hand and slide my glasses up onto my head so I can see it properly.

It's me and Billie, last night on the red carpet. She's in my arms like the prize she is, and a smile that's probably never been seen before is all over my face.

Shit.

"What about it?" I ask, handing it back to him like it's no big deal, when in reality it's a really big god damn deal.

"Don't fucking try that shit with me. I know you, Masen, known you since we were eleven years old – don't bullshit me. We've been friends – fuck that, *brothers* – for twelve years and I've never seen you look that happy."

"I've never had to work on my public image before now."

He scowls at me, and I drop my shades back down to hide my eyes from him, because he's fucking right – absolutely one hundred percent correct – I've never looked at anything or anyone the way I'm looking at Billie in that picture.

Not even when my albums made it to platinum, or I sold out massive arenas, not when my songs were number one hits or I made millions of dollars. No, instead I reserve my smiles for a too-sweet fucking girl dropping an f bomb.

I don't know what the hell is wrong with me.

I grab a cigarette from my box and light it up, trying desperately to calm my nerves.

I want to talk to him about it, because he's right about us being like brothers too – he's the only person that has stuck by my side when things turned from bad to ugly, but I can't. I just can't.

"It's not real, bro," I lie instead. "We're just playing our parts."

"Whatever you say, man, believe that if it helps you sleep at night... but you don't fool me."

He strips off his shirt and charges full steam towards the pool.

Motherfucker.

***

"Sugar, come with me."

She rolls her head to the side, glancing at me over her bare shoulder.

"Only if you tell me where we're going?"

I tip my head and start walking away – she'll follow, I know she will.

I grin to myself as I hear her feet padding across the hard wood flooring behind me, muttering words I can't make out.

I glance at her over my shoulder as I reach the doorway for the stairs and her eyes widen in surprise.

She follows me down the stairs, past the bowling lane and into my studio. I can practically hear her curiosity screaming at me the entire way.

I turn to face her, my heart thumping.

I've never done anything even remotely close to this before, but here I am, breaking all the fucking rules for this girl.

She stops when she sees me stop, and her brow furrows as she tries to figure out what she's doing here.

"Sit." I point at the couch and she complies, lowering her lithe body onto the seat without argument.

My gaze holds on her longer than it should, and I have to tear myself away before I can get the message to my brain that this is a really bad idea.

I stride across the room and take the brand new, acoustic guitar off the wall. I'm passing it to her and she's holding it before she can question what it's for.

I sink down onto the stool in front of her, my lyric sheet in my subtly shaking hands.

"What are you doing?" she whispers, holding the instrument like it's a loaded fucking bomb.

"Sing with me."

Her eyes widen as she looks from the guitar, to me, and then back again.

"Oh, no, Mase... I don't... I don't sing."

"You sing."

Her face pales. "I barely even play," she whispers.

"Do you trust me?" I ask her, and for the first time in my life, the answer to a simple question scares me.

She's still for a few beats, but when she nods her head, I release a breath I didn't know I'd been holding.

My nerves are shot to shit right now. I need a smoke, but surprisingly, I don't feel like I need a drink.

In fact, now that I think about it, I haven't truly craved a drink ever since that night at the bar.

The same night I slept with Billie.

I shake the thought out of my head. There's no connection there, my mind is doing what it always does – fucking with me.

"Then trust me, sugar. Sing with me. *Play*."

I pass her the music, and she takes it, her eyes barely glancing over it before she sets it aside – she should know the melody already – she created it.

Her fingers tentatively grip the glossy guitar in her hands, and I take that as my cue to reach for mine, sitting it in my lap and strumming her in.

She joins me, effortlessly, like we've been playing together for years.

I swallow deeply as we reach the intro to the first verse.

I go for it, pouring all my confusion over my feelings into the words. She holds back, but her eyes don't once leave mine as I hit the second verse and then the chorus.

I've given up on hearing her voice again when she opens her mouth and the beautiful melody falls from her sexy lips, weaving effortlessly with the huskiness of mine.

I stumble over a few words, in shock, and she smiles shyly.

My heart rate speeds up as we float through the rest of the chorus, I belt out the verses and my fingers still on the strings.

Billie is breathing rapidly, her shoulders rising and falling as she stares at the ground, taking a minute.

I know how she feels. I could take a million minutes right now and it still wouldn't be enough.

I've just bared my fucking soul to a woman who is being paid to be my girlfriend. I've shared more of myself with her than I have anyone else and I don't know what the hell to make of that.

She finally looks up at me, her hazel eyes soft and dreamy.

Beautiful.

Frightening.

Real.

Fuck.

Josh was right.

I'm not fooling anyone, not even myself, which means I'm probably doing a pretty piss poor job of keeping Billie on the right side of the walls I've built up over the years.

I need to get a handle on this, and I need to do it now.

"That was incredible, Mase. Seriously, I love it."

I nod, but otherwise ignore the compliment. I've never been good with those.

She flashes me a confused expression as I sit my guitar back on the stand before taking hers and laying it on the floor.

I rake my hand down my face and then through my hair.

I don't know how to say this, or why I feel so fucking sick over it, but I know for sure that it has to be done.

"Do you remember when I told you that I couldn't give you anything but sex, sugar? Do you remember that?"

She nods, her fingers crossing and uncrossing in her lap. "I remember."

"I just ah..." I drag my hand through my hair again. "Shit, I don't know, I just wanted to make sure that you were still good with that."

Hurt flashes through her eyes, but it's gone as quickly as it came.

"I'm not trying to be an asshole, I just... Chuck wanted to make sure we were sticking to the plan," I lie.

She studies me carefully, her gaze so intense I have to look away.

She gets to her feet, and it takes everything in me not to stand with her.

I know I've just hurt her – badly – after what we just did, the music we just made together, the bond we shared – for me to then go and cut it off at the knees might just be the most ruthless thing I've ever done in my life.

"Yeah, of course we're good," she answers brightly – too fucking brightly. "We're totally fine. Tell Chuck not to worry. I know what's at stake."

She takes a few steps towards the door and my hand aches to reach out and stop her, but I don't. I'm frozen.

"I've gotta go meet Avery. I need to go." The words are weighted, calculated.

Fucking hell. What have I done?

This feels like goodbye.

"Are you coming back?" I ask, calling her on her bullshit reassurances, and hating the spike in my heartrate as I wait to hear her reply.

"Honestly?" she whispers.

I nod.

"I'm not sure."

I don't even get a chance to reply before she's gone.

CHAPTER EIGHTEEN

Billie

I will not cry.

I will not cry.

I will not cry.

I repeat the words over and over to myself like a mantra as I drive over to Avery's – *my* – apartment.

I shouldn't be surprised that Masen served me a reality check, he can probably see by taking one look at me that I'm in too deep.

I should have been able to see that it was totally one sided.

I should have believed him when he told me that this thing between us would be sex and nothing more, but like a fool, I *hoped*.

The streets fly by in a blur and before I know it, I'm turning into my usual parking space and killing the engine of my piece-of-shit car.

I managed to slip out without Eric seeing, so for the first time in the past month or two, I actually got to drive myself somewhere without supervision.

I'm out of the car and up the stairs, my feet echoing against the metal with every step.

Giggling fills the air as I open the door and I hear Josh's booming voice teasing Avery about something.

I stop for a minute, leaning my back against the door after I close it quietly. I just want to listen to the two of them for a minute.

It might not be anything serious yet, but when I see them together, laughing and joking, touching and kissing, it makes me jealous.

"B?" Avery calls out when she hears my keys drop onto the bench.

"Just me."

"What are you doing here?"

I follow their voices into her bedroom and find the two of them, each half-dressed, a poker game laid out on the bed between them.

I lean against the door frame and laugh at Josh's wolfish grin.

"Strip poker, you two? Really?"

Josh waggles his brows suggestively. "You wanna join us, FG?"

Avery smacks his arm, grinning. "Don't even try it. Masen will kick your ass."

My smile falls at the mention of his name and it doesn't go unnoticed by my best friend.

"Uh oh."

"What?" I ask, plastering a fake smile on my lips.

"Oh no, that pained-looking face doesn't fool me, I saw it. Trouble in fake paradise?"

I bounce my eyes between Josh and Avery before settling on the floor.

"Shit," Avery hisses.

"What?" Josh asks, his tone hushed.

"Your boy fucked up somehow, that's *what*," she replies, her tone accusing, as though Josh is somehow partly to blame.

I look up to see the pair of them climbing off her bed.

Josh shrugs his shirt over his head and approaches me slowly, his expression unreadable.

"What'd he do, FG?"

I drop my chin, but he doesn't allow it, cupping my jaw in his big hand, forcing me to look at him.

"Nothing," I breathe.

"FG," he warns, and I'm sucked in by his tone and big blue eyes.

He's a sweet guy. A part of me wishes it could be him that I loved – loving Josh wouldn't be easy, but it wouldn't be this hard either.

"He just... we were singing together and then... I dunno... it was nothing," I ramble and Josh frowns, stooping to get level with me, pinning me with his stare.

"You sang together?"

I nod.

"That's, wow, that's new."

I feel a flicker of hope at his shock, but it's short-lived when I think about Masen breaking my heart right afterwards.

"Then what happened?"

"He just reminded me of our arrangement. You know, sex without strings..."

Josh's head falls forward and he mutters something under his breath.

I'm really going to miss being his friend if this is all over.

"It's fine. I'm fine with it, I just... wanted to come and hang out with Avery for a bit. Everything is fine."

"I think the fact that you just said fine three times, is a pretty good indicator that *nothing* is fine," Avery pipes up.

"Just... don't give up on him yet, FG, okay?" he pleads.

I shrug my shoulders. I'm not sure how to respond to that.

"I gotta go, babe," Josh says, stepping away from me, talking to Avery. "Let you two have some girl time, alright?"

They exchange a kiss that makes my heart ache, and then he's gone.

***

"Sit. Talk. I'll make coffee," she instructs.

I flop onto the couch, dragging a big squishy cushion into my lap.

"I don't even know where to start."

"Start with *how* you fell in love with a guy who only ever scowls," she yells from the kitchen.

"I'm not in love with him," I snap.

Lie. *Total lie.*

"*Whatever*, just start at our weekend away, what the hell happened there? One minute he's got some chick in his lap and the next he's carrying you off to his bedroom to have his way with you."

I grin and sink my teeth into my bottom lip to try and control it. I shouldn't be smiling, certainly not about the other girl, but I can't help it. It was the first time I felt brave enough to really tell him what I wanted, and when you're dealing with someone like Masen Lennox, that's no small thing.

"I'm sure we've already been over this."

"Humour me," she insists as she appears in the doorway with two steaming cups of coffee. "You tried telling me about it, but every time we got going, Mr. Tall, Dark and Broody appeared.

"I finally grew some balls and told him I wasn't going to do this with him if he was just going to run all over town sleeping with whoever he felt like."

She sits, passing me my cup.

"Okay, so you had sex, right?"

I want to correct her, tell her that the simple phrase is in no way sufficient to explain what it was like when the two of us finally came together, but I just nod in agreement.

"And then?"

"And then today he reminds me that it's just sex, no strings – like he told me in the beginning, and I'm just the fool who's feeling things when she was warned not to."

Her eyes fill with sadness.

"Have you been sleeping together since we got back?"

"Every night." I shrug.

"Wow," she whispers.

My eyes rise from my cup to meet hers. "What?"

She shrugs. "Nothing."

I pin her with my stare.

"Fine, it was just something Josh told me about Masen and his... *activities*."

I cringe. I don't know why – I'm well aware that Masen has been with women before me, probably more women than I'd like to think about.

"Just say it."

She shoots me a sympathetic look. "Josh said that Masen has never screwed the same girl twice."

I frown. "Like two nights in a row?"

She shakes her head. "Like ever."

"But... I..." I stutter. "I don't get it."

She looks at me knowingly. "He doesn't go back for seconds, B, it's just sex and then it's done, and he moves on with his life. He never lets women stay the night in a hotel, let alone in his home."

"He told me it was just sex too, those were his words."

"But that's not what he's shown you."

"This is a unique situation," I argue, unwilling to believe that I could possibly be the exception for him when he just so brutally shut me down.

"Yeah, because of you... you know what Josh thinks?"

I clasp my cup, trying to warm my suddenly chilly hands. "I wouldn't dare try to figure out what goes on in that boy's head."

She smiles softly and I see it, she's falling – hard. "He thinks Masen has feelings for you."

"And what do you think?"

She shrugs her shoulders. "I don't know what to make of that man. He confuses me. He's harsh and cold, but sometimes when he looks at you, I think I see another side of him."

"He's different sometimes. I've seen a part of him that I never would have believed was there. Last night at the premiere, I don't know, Avery, it was so easy to believe he loved me back."

"I told you that you loved him."

I roll my eyes. "Fine, okay, you were right, I'm in love with him. I'm fucking obsessed."

She giggles, but there's a wariness in her eyes.

"He was sweet, considerate, charming."

"What if it was all an act, B?"

I release a deep breath. I've worried about the same thing.

"But what if it wasn't? What if that was the real him?"

I could go back and forth like this all day. My head is a mess.

She shrugs again – neither of us have any answers.

"I have to try."

"I'm just worried he's going to break your heart."

He's already cracked it, but it's not completely broken – not yet.

I'm worried too, but I get the feeling that I'm too far in to care – getting your heart stomped on by Masen would be soul destroying, but at the same time, so, so worth it if it meant getting to be close to him for even a moment longer.

"Me too, but you know what the saddest thing is? I'm not sure I care. I went into this thing with my eyes wide open."

"That doesn't mean that you could see everything that was coming."

My protest dies on my lips. She's right, I couldn't see it coming, but I'm here now and I can't change that.

"Just be careful, Billie, I love you and I don't want to see him break you."

I reach out and squeeze her hand.

She's right to be concerned, this is nothing but a mess that's bound to end in heartbreak, but she doesn't see what I see when I look at him – she only sees the broken pieces of him, but I see the way they're begging to be put back together.

Now I just have to figure out if I'm strong enough to try and be his glue.

CHAPTER NINETEEN

Masen

I strum the guitar that I bought for her in my hands. I didn't even tell her that it was hers.

I didn't tell her anything that wasn't total bullshit.

I lift the instrument, my fingers twitching to throw it across the room, but I don't – not this. Any other object in this room would be sailing through the air by now, crashing against the wall and smashing into a million pieces, but I can't bring myself to destroy another piece of her.

"What's up, asshole?"

I startle, spinning in my chair to look at Josh. Can't believe I didn't hear the big bastard coming.

"Who would have fucking believed that you could be quiet when you wanted to."

He drops onto the couch, his arms splaying wide, his eyes not giving me a moment's reprieve from the glare he's sporting.

I pick at the strings, waiting him out.

I only get halfway through the second verse when he pipes up.

"I was just with Avery."

I nod, not looking up. That means he's seen Billie.

I hear him blow out a breath. "Look, man..."

My hands still and my eyes slowly rise. I might not like what he's about to say, but I owe him the respect of looking in his eyes while he says it.

"You know I think of you like a brother... but that girl? She's something special, and the way you're treating her? It's not okay." He pauses for a beat. "She's hurting, bro, and you clearly are too."

Fuck.

A pained expression crosses my face. I never wanted to hurt her, that's the whole point of this fucking arrangement – so *she* doesn't get hurt.

He continues, either oblivious to the weight settling on my chest as I start to get crushed, bit by bit, or just not giving a fuck. "As much as I can see she loves you, you need to let her go – she's too good for this version of you."

"She doesn't love me," I growl.

She can't. She might feel something for me, but not love – it can't be love.

"She's not here selling fucking girl scout cookies," he snaps, exasperated.

I level him with a stare. "She does *not* love me," I say through clenched teeth.

"Fuck's sake, Masen, she loves you so much it's hard to watch." He runs his hand through his blond hair. "I'm not going to argue with you about it, but if you can't love her back, then you need to let her go – money, reputation, career be damned, she deserves to have someone love her."

"Someone like *you*?" I sneer, my jealously finally rearing its ugly head.

"I'm going to pretend you didn't just say that."

"Why?" I demand, pushing myself from asshole into complete-and-utter-prick territory. "You were into her the moment you laid eyes on her."

He laughs humourlessly, his jaw ticking. "You know what's funny? You think you see so much – *everything* – but you can't even see that you're crazy about her. It'd be funny if it wasn't so god damn tragic."

I don't have a reply for that, instead I reach into my pocket, pull out a cigarette and light it up, right here in my studio.

He gets to his feet, his disappointment evident. "I'm out."

"What would you know about love anyway?" I ask his back.

"I know more about it than you'd think."

I huff out a breath. He doesn't know shit about love. Sure, he has parents, a family that love him and he loves back – but the love he's talking about – *falling in love...* He doesn't know fuck all about that.

"You take some chick out on a few dates and suddenly you're in love?" I push.

"She's not just some chick. I'm going to marry that girl, mark my words. I'm a changed man." He turns, a serene smile on his face that guts me more than his disappointment in me.

He believes everything he's saying, and for a split second, I wish I could feel the same way.

"I don't know what goes on in that head of yours, Masen, but you're your own worst enemy." He sighs.

I nod in agreement as he leaves, and the moment he's gone, I grab my guitar and snap it over my thigh, the wood splintering and cracking – a pretty fucking accurate representation of my cold, black heart right now.

Fuck.

***

My hand hovers over the bottle of scotch, my head warring with me.

I know I shouldn't do it, *fuck* – I know it, but she was my fix, and I fucked it all up.

Nothing new there.

That's why I need the drink – not because she's my fix, but because she's *gone,* and I have no idea if she's ever coming back.

That's on my shoulders. I did that.

I made her come here in one breath and then in another I forced her to leave.

I uncap the bottle and lift it slowly to my nose so I can breathe in the all-too-familiar scent.

My mouth waters as the sweet scent fills my nose.

"I'll drink you down, you'd burn so good."

A line from my new song floats through my mind and I slam the bottle down.

I can't do it. No matter how badly I might want to.

My hands shake as I carry it to the sink and empty it – the one and only remaining bottle of alcohol in this entire house, a ten-thousand-dollar bottle of scotch – literally down the drain.

I can't get out of my ensuite bathroom and back into my bedroom fast enough.

"Jesus Christ." I drop my face into my hands – shaken by how damn close I just came to screwing it all up all over again.

"Good choice." Her soft voice comes from behind me and I spin around – caught off guard for the second time today. She's watching my every move.

"You came back."

The words are hanging in the air between us before I can contemplate how desperate and fucking stupid they sound.

She nods slowly. "I came back, and I'll be here until you tell me to leave."

She's lingering in the doorway of my bedroom and as much as I was craving that bottle of booze, it has nothing on how badly I want to close the distance between me and this woman.

She's an addiction of the most terrifying kind.

"I'm sorry," I say. Two words that have never crossed my lips before this moment.

"For what?" she questions, her head tilting to study me carefully.

She's asking me the question, but she already knows the answer – I can see it in her hazel eyes.

I shrug, always the asshole.

"Masen," she breathes, her tone begging.

I don't know what she's asking me for – I don't know how to be what she's looking for.

She steps into my room, and I lose the last of my self-control.

She sighs as I eat up the distance between us and hold her tight against my body. I might be all fucked up, but I know one thing, it seems like less of a big deal when she's around.

She presses the side of her face against my chest – her hands gripping onto my shirt like she's afraid this is all going to be over soon.

"I need to tell you something," she whispers, and my heart rate accelerates further.

Nothing good ever follows a sentence that begins like that.

She pulls back, tipping her head up so she can look right at my face.

Her palm settles over my racing heart and I sink into her touch. It's not enough, it's never going to be enough, but I don't know how to get more.

"What is it, sugar?" I murmur, terrified of the answer.

She looks scared, and I don't blame her, she should be scared. What she's about to say has the power to break me. I can feel it.

"I love you – I'm in love with you, Mase," she whispers.

A feeling of dread rips though me – it must take my facial features with it because she pulls away like I've physically slapped her.

"No," I growl as I pace. "No, no, no."

I sink down onto the edge of my bed, my head in my hands. "Fuck."

"Masen, look at me," she pleads, dropping to crouch in front of me.

I can't do it. I can't look at her.

Josh was right.

She fucking loves me, and I'm going to destroy her because I'm not capable of loving her back.

No matter what I do now, she hurts.

She hurts because of me.

I need to make her leave before this goes any further, just like he said. That would be the best thing for her, the *kindest*, but the idea of setting her free for someone else to claim makes my hands shake.

I don't know what I'm meant to do without her.

She tugs at my hands, trying to pull them from my face, but she can't make them budge an inch.

"Look at me, Masen," she demands. "Look at me and tell me you don't feel something for me too."

I feel *something* – I know I do. But it's not enough, it's not *everything*. It's not what someone else could give her. It's not what she deserves.

"Masen, please," she whispers, tears threatening her voice.

I want her. I want her so badly I don't know how I'll breathe without her, but I can't risk this – not with *her*.

This is her heart on the line.

She's offering me her heart, and if you give someone that, you give them the power to crush you.

I can't be the person responsible for doing that to her. Not my sugar.

She's good.

Sweet.

Perfect.

Mine. My brain tells me, but I ignore it.

I lower my hands, and she breathes a sigh of relief as our eyes meet, but it'll be short-lived – I know that much.

"I told you, sugar, it was just sex," I say, doing my fucking best to keep her from seeing the anguish on the inside.

She frowns, but she's not giving up – not yet.

"But that was before," she says softly.

"Before *what*?" I ask lazily, like this isn't the most fucked up moment of my life.

"Before *us*," she says, her tone rising.

"There is no us." I get to my feet, the volume of my voice rising with me. "There. Is. No. Us. There was just *fucking*, plain and simple."

She scrambles to get to her feet, and my girl is strong, because she matches me toe to toe – not backing down for a second.

"Fuck that, Masen, I know it was more than that. I know *you*, you just have to let me in."

"Whatever you think you know is a lie. Just like this relationship. You're just a girl who's being paid to be here."

Raw, real hurt crosses her face, and I hate myself for it.

"I want you to go, Billie. I'm telling you to leave."

She nods slowly, over and over again. "Alright. I get it. I see what you're doing, and I just want you to acknowledge that this isn't me leaving you – I'm not your parents, Mase – I'm not leaving you – *you're* pushing me away. Okay? And for the record, I don't want your money... you can keep it."

She takes a step back, and I have to physically stop myself from pulling her back closer.

"Whatever," I mutter, my voice cracking, betraying me.

She turns her back on me, turning before she gets out the door.

"You know what? This *won't* work. You can't stop people from loving you. You might not be able to accept my love, but it hasn't stopped me from giving it to you anyway."

My heart pounds as she disappears from sight, closing the door softly behind her.

CHAPTER TWENTY

Tears spill down my cheeks as I run down the stairs towards 'my room'. I want to slam the door but I won't give him the satisfaction, instead closing it the same way I did his – like he hasn't just ripped my heart clean out of my chest.

I throw myself onto my bed and let it all come out – the hurt, frustration, anger... it all spills onto my pillows in waves.

I want to hate him, but hate is a hard thing to feel for the man I left upstairs.

I *love* him – plain and simple, but more than that, I feel for him so deeply that I can see past his hurtful words.

His pain destroys me. He gets cut and I'm the one who bleeds.

He truly believes he's alone in this world.

He's accepted that Josh is here, but I don't think he'd be surprised if one day he just stopped turning up for him, and that's after twelve years – I've only been here five minutes.

He's never been able to rely on anyone or anything for most of his life and that breaks my heart far more than any of the lies he just told me ever could.

I wrap my arms around myself, I feel like I'm being torn in half.

I couldn't make these feelings go away even if I tried, but I can't make him let me in either.

That's the real sick part of it.

You can't make someone do something they don't want to do – even if you know it's something good for them.

I pick up my cell phone and type out a message to Avery.

To: Avery
From: Billie
He pushed me away and it really fucking hurts.

Admitting that to my best friend brings on a fresh wave of tears. I swipe them away, angry at myself for being so sensitive to something I should have seen coming a mile away.

My phone dings.

To: Billie
From: Avery
I'm so sorry, babe, want me to come over?

I shake my head – not that she can see, but I just want to be alone in my misery.

What I really want to do is pack my bags and get the fuck out of here for good – he told me to leave after all, but the idea of not coming back here – not seeing him every single day makes my chest ache.

I'm not ready for that – not yet at least.

There's a knock at my door and I fly off the bed, rushing to answer it in the hopes it might be him.

I fling open the door and when it's Morris standing there and not Masen, my stomach clenches.

"Morris, sorry, I thought it might have been...."

"Sorry, Miss Tatum, I didn't mean to disrupt you."

He reaches out like he might pat my shoulder, but thinks twice about it, his hand dropping awkwardly. It gets a small smile out of me. He's the sweetest.

"It's fine, Morris, did you need something?"

My stomach tightens. He's probably here to carry my bags out for me.

He has to do all of the shitty jobs for Masen, and I bet evicting his fake girlfriend is one of them.

He opens his mouth to explain, but I cut him off.

"I'll just get started on the packing now and I should be out of your hair in about half an hour, is that okay?"

He frowns at me, confused. "I don't mean to sound foolish, but where are you going?"

It's my turn to frown now. "Home." He still looks confused, so I continue, "He didn't send you to move me out?"

He shakes his head quickly. "No, Miss Tatum, he did not. I haven't spoken to him."

"Maybe he just hasn't had time to ask you –"

He interrupts me. "It's not my place to say, but girlfriends weren't exactly covered in my contract and if I'm honest, you're the first one he's had, so please excuse me if I'm overstepping my boundaries here, but I don't think Mr. Lennox wants you to go at all, in fact, I think he's just crying out for you to stay."

"I'm not really his girlfriend," I correct him.

"I'm aware of what you are to him," he says, his old eyes knowingly looking into mine. "He might not have figured it out yet, but he just needs a little push."

"I think I pushed pretty hard," I admit. "It might be the problem."

"Give it one more shove," he says, and then without another word about my impending departure, he turns and walks away.

I watch him leave with a mixture of confusion and unease.

He doesn't want me to give up on Masen. Truthfully, I don't want to give up on him either, I don't want to be another person on the long list of people that have let him down in his life.

I want to be more.

I want to be *his*.

***

I pause outside his bedroom door. I don't know what the hell I'm thinking – I'm not up for another round of that.

One more hurtful word and I'm going to cry in front of him, and I hate the idea of letting him see how weak he's made me, but it's nothing compared to the thought of him thinking I've walked out on him.

He needs me. I just have to trust that he feels what I'm feeling.

I turn the handle slowly and gently push open the door.

A whimper slips from between my lips as I take in his form, sitting on the floor, his back against the bed, knees bent, elbows resting on them and his face in his hands.

He snaps around in my direction as he hears me, and something sparks in his eyes that has me rushing across the room and dropping at his side.

His expression is tortured. He's hurting.

I'm crying now, my plans of staying strong and hiding my feelings from him, long forgotten.

"Masen," I rasp, my voice thick.

He doesn't answer, just drops his face back down again as I wrap my arms around his shoulders.

He stills for a beat, and I prepare myself for the rejection, but it doesn't come. Instead he lifts his head, breathes in deeply and murmurs, "Sugar."

"I'm here," I promise. "I won't give up on you."

"Sugar," he repeats, the anguish in his tone chipping away another piece of my heart. "I'm sorry I hurt you."

"*Mase*," I whisper. "Let me love you."

He reacts then, tugging me into his arms and onto his lap, holding me so tight I can barely breathe.

We sit like that for what feels like forever, clinging onto one another like we're the only thing the other can count on – and maybe in a way, we are.

His face lifts from my neck, slowly, and *finally* I get to see those beautiful, haunted, eyes.

"I want you, sugar, I just don't know how to be enough for you."

Fresh tears slip from my eyes. He wants me. He said it aloud.

"You're already enough."

"I'm *nothing*. You deserve *everything*."

I run my fingers across his jaw, my twisted, damaged man.

"You couldn't be nothing if you tried."

His eyes fall to the floor and I follow, seeing the open folder and its contents spread out next to him for the first time.

"What's all this?"

"It's you, in a folder."

I frown, but my eyes scan over the contents. My class schedules, lists of names from my classes... even the name of the boy I dated last year... my teachers... *everything*. It's all there.

Me in a folder.

"I don't understand."

He shrugs, his dark eyes finding me again. "I had to know. I needed to know everything about you, and it was driving me insane because I had no idea why I even cared."

"You can ask me anything, Masen. I'll tell you anything."

He nods, and I can tell that information pleases him.

I run my fingers through his hair, and he leans into my touch.

"You care because you love me too," I break it to him gently, afraid that he'll bolt on me again.

"Billie, I can't... I don't know how to..."

I silence him, pressing my finger to his lips. "I don't need the words, Masen, I've got you."

"You're too good for me, sugar."

I don't know how to make him see how untrue that is. Time, I guess. I'll give him time and one day he'll stop doubting.

I'll give him *everything*, and all he'll have to do is learn to take it from me.

"I love you, Masen Lennox, and you're just going to have to deal with that."

He smiles, a tiny, barely-there twitch of his lips, but it's enough for me – *he's* enough for me.

"I'm an addict, Billie."

I know exactly what and who he is. There's nothing he can say that's going to change my mind.

"I think I might be addicted to you," he whispers, and I grin.

I'm sure it's terribly unhealthy, but I don't give a shit.

"Then I must be an addict too, because I'm sure as hell addicted to you."

I see the words ticking over in his brain.

"I wrote you a song," he murmurs, and I think this is probably the first time he's admitted what I already know.

That song is for me.

That song is his way of telling me how he feels.

"I know." I giggle.

"It's about you," he confesses.

"I know it is."

He smiles, a fraction wider this time, and just for me.

"I had the guitar you were playing made for you."

This time I am surprised. "You did?"

"Just for you, sugar."

My heart thumps rapidly. He's a man of few words, but the ones he does choose, steal my breath.

I take him by surprise, crashing our lips together in a flurry of passion and promise.

He might not be a prince charming – not even close – but he's the only fairy-tale I need.

He's my happily ever after, as fucked up as it might turn out to be.

We break apart, his forehead resting against mine and when he starts to softly sing to me – *my song* – I melt.

He might not be able to say those three little words to me, but he shows me how he feels, even if he doesn't know it.

Like right now, as he croons quietly in my ear, he *sings* his love to me.

There are twenty-six letters in the alphabet. You can arrange those letters into a seemingly endless number of words, but no matter the outcome, no matter what words he chooses, all I hear when he sings, is love.

EPILOGUE

I can't believe I'm fucking doing this.

There's not a single person in the world that could convince me this was a good idea, other than the drop-dead fucking gorgeous one at my side.

I scowl at her as she pokes out her tongue.

The reporter looks at the interaction between us and smiles the same way people do when they look at puppies. Like we're *cute* or some bullshit.

"So, how long have the two of you been together?"

"A year," I answer at the same time that Billie says, "About nine months."

I smirk.

I count from the moment I first saw her, that first day at the office. She counts from the day I finally admitted that I wanted her.

We exchange a look, but neither of us bother to correct the other, nor do we explain the difference in dates.

"Ooookay." She notes down the two separate figures.

"Billie, what do you do for a living?"

That'll score big points with my girl. The only thing she hates more than my smoking habit, is people assuming that she just mooches off me.

"I'm just finishing my degree right now, but I've been helping out with the production side of Masen's new album with the record label and they've offered me a position with them when I'm finished school."

She smiles brightly and my chest fucking bursts with pride.

She's got talent by the bucket load.

Saying she 'helped' is the vastest understatement I've ever heard. She could have single-handedly produced my entire album herself, but like the god damn angel she is, she was happy to take a back seat and pretend the suits there knew something she didn't.

They certainly don't know how to play guitar and sing backup for me – but my girl does – with a bit of shameless begging on my behalf.

"Masen, your friend Josh was just telling me what a changed man you are since you and Billie got together, do you care to comment on that?"

I shoot daggers at Josh, who's lounging over the other side of the pool and Billie giggles.

"Josh is kind of a shit-stirring moron," Billie explains.

"Hey! I resent that," Josh yells across at her.

"If the slipper fits," Billie mutters under her breath.

"So, you don't think he's a changed man?" the reporter questions curiously, her attention on my girl.

Billie shrugs as she glances at me. "He's his own man. I can't take credit for that level of perfection."

Josh makes gagging sounds from his spot, and I flip him off.

"You're too fucking sweet, sugar," I say, my voice gruff.

The reporter, Jane I think she said her name was, sighs, her eyes soft and dreamy.

That's my cue that I need to get the hell out of dodge.

"I need a swim," I announce, stripping my t-shirt off over my head and reaching for my cigarettes.

Billie's hand lands on top of mine and squeezes tight. She shakes her head.

I hold back a groan. She's worn me down on a lot of things in the months since she officially moved in, but she's yet to crack me on the smokes – but it's not through lack of trying.

"Well thank you for your time, Masen, I really appreciate it."

I nod at her in response.

Fucking Billie.

I don't do interviews. Definitely don't let reporters in my house, but sugar insisted that we bend the rules one time, and if I've learnt one thing this past year, it's that I'm shitty at telling that girl no.

I release the pack of cigarettes with a huff and she smiles victoriously.

I stroll towards the pool, feeling two sets of eyes on me.

Billie finally wore me down on this too – apparently my girl likes me shirtless and dripping wet, so this was one thing I was all too happy to fold on.

"So, I'll see you at the shoot next week?" Jane calls after me, and I pause on the edge of the pool. "Photoshoot? For the calendar?" she replies, confused.

"He'll be there," Josh tells her at the same moment that Billie nods furiously.

Fuck.

I don't know what they're up to, but it's bound to be bad news for me.

"Tell me now and make it quick." I point a finger at Billie.

She shoots me a sheepish expression. "You know I can't say no when people ask for things."

"Then stop answering my phone, sugar, because no is the only answer I give."

"It's just one little photo." She winces. "Shirtless."

I raise my brows.

"It's for sick kids..."

She knows that won't sway me – I already give a shit load of money to charity – they don't need a half-naked photo of me too.

She scrunches up her nose. Her soft eyes begging and, *hell*, I'll do it. This woman owns me.

I might not be the kind of man to tell her I love her every day, but she knows it. She knows she owns every part of me.

"Beckett Thorn is doing it," she barters, and I chuckle.

"That's the best bargaining point you've got, sugar?"

"That's the best I've got." She throws her hands up in defeat.

"Fine. I'll do it."

She fist-pumps the air.

"But I'm going to be smoking in the photo."

I catch her scowl and hear Josh's chuckle before I leap into the pool, probably covering them in water.

I grin as I swim towards the surface. She's standing on the side, hands on her hips, trying her hardest, and failing not to smile at me.

My sugar, she's too damn sweet.

OTHER TITLES

Love like Yours Series
Rushed – Book 1
Pierced – Book 2
Hunted – Book 3
Chased – Book 4

Rock Games Novels
Paper, Scissors, Rock: Vol. 1
Hide and Seek: Vol. 2

My Heart Duet
My Heart Needs
My Heart Wants

Calendar Boys Novels
Mr. January
Mr. February
Mr. March
Mr. April
Mr. May
Mr. June
Mr. July
Mr. August
Mr. September

Mr. October

ACKNOWLEDGEMENTS

The songs that inspired this book: *Wild Love (Acoustic)* – James Bay, *Just For Tonight* – James Bay, and *Tearin' Up My Heart* – Kina Grannis.

I really loved writing about Masen and Billie – I know I shouldn't have favourites between my book babies, but I think this one might be my favourite of the series (so far at least).

I hope you all enjoyed Masen and Billie as much as I do.

I can't believe I'm getting down to the end of the series already, this year has just flown by so fast. Thank you all for the support of these books, it means the worlds to me!

Stacey and Bianca, thank you for being as excited about by asshole rocker as I am!

ABOUT THE AUTHOR

NICOLE S. GOODIN is a romance author and mother of two from Taranaki in the North Island of New Zealand.

In mid-2015, she started to write about a group of characters who wouldn't get out of her head. Her first book, Rushed, was published in mid-2016.

Nicole enjoys long walks on the beach, pillow fights and braiding her friends' hair. She dislikes clichés, talking about herself in the third person, and people who don't understand her sense of humour.

Please feel free to contact her either via her website, email, Instagram, Twitter or on her Facebook page, she would love to hear your feedback. If you're feeling really game, you can even sign up for her newsletter.

Visit www.nicolegoodinauthor.com for more information.

UPCOMING TITLES

Calendar Boys Novels

179

Mr. November
Mr. December